PRAISE FOR THE SERIES

"The perfect mystery to read with a glass of vino in hand."

—*Shelf Awareness,* starred review

"Light and enjoyable… If you feel like taking an armchair tour of France, they hit just the right spot."

—*Mystery Scene Magazine*

"Masterful."

—*Star Tribune*

"Beautifully done."

—*Bookloons*

"Decadent, delicious, and delightful, The Winemaker Detective series blends an immersion in French countryside, winemaking and gourmet attitude with mystery and intrigue."

—*Wine Industry Network Advisor*

"A fun and informative take on the cozy crime mystery, French style."

—*Eurocrime*

Cognac Conspiracies

The heirs to one of the oldest Cognac estates in France face a hostile takeover by foreign investors. The Winemaker Detective is called in to audit the books and has his loyalties tested.

Mayhem in Margaux

A heat wave has local vintners on edge, but the Winemaker Detective is focused on solving a mystery that touches him very personally and leads him to uncover the shady side of a grand cru classé wine.

Flambé in Armagnac

The Winemaker Detective heads to Gascony, where a fire has ravaged the warehouse of one of the region's finest Armagnac producers, and a small town holds fiercely onto its secrets.

Montmartre Mysteries

The Winemaker Detective visits a favorite wine shop in Paris and stumbles upon an attempted murder, drawing him into investigation that leads them from the Foreign Legion to the Côte du Rhône.

Backstabbing in Beaujolais

Can the Winemaker Detective and his assistant keep calculating real estate agents, taciturn winegrowers, dubious wine merchants and suspicious deaths from delaying delivery of the world-famous Beaujolais Nouveau?

Late Harvest Havoc

Disaster strikes the vineyards in Alsace. Vintners are tense and old grudges surface. The Winemaker Detective's reputation is on the line and he must find the cause before the late harvest starts.

Tainted Tokay

A Winemaker Detective Mystery

Jean-Pierre Alaux and Noël Balen

Translated by Sally Pane

LE FRENCH BOOK

Wine is sunlight, held together by water.
　　　　　　　　　　　　　—Galileo

1

"Florence, I'd envy your life in this immense château if it weren't for the ghosts. I'm sure you have one or two lurking in there," Benjamin Cooker said as he dropped a packet of artificial sweetener in his coffee.

"Benjamin, you always surprise me. I would have never guessed that France's most celebrated authority in matters of winemaking would be superstitious."

Benjamin sipped his coffee and tried not to grimace at the bitter taste of the sweetener. Elisabeth was nagging him to lose weight again, and he had reluctantly given up sugar in his coffee to please his wife.

"Do you, of all people, really believe in ghosts?" Florence Blanchard continued.

"That would depend on what kind of ghost you're talking about. If you mean a disembodied soul, well, I do believe in the soul. It's the seat of life and intelligence itself."

Florence nodded. "That's one way of looking at it, I suppose. If I recall correctly, the Marquise de Deffand, the famous seventeenth-century hostess, was asked once of she believed in ghosts. She answered, 'No, but I'm afraid of them.'"

"I have to say that I'm more afraid of the living and our small-mindedness, which leads to so much deception and duplicity. To respond to your quote, I'll cite Pierre Corneille, who said, 'Deceit is a game of petty spirits'—those are the ghosts I fear."

Sitting in the garden with his host, Benjamin looked up and studied the small cupola atop the château's slate roof. The morning sun was blazing down on the mansion, bleaching its Charente-stone exterior.

Dating to the 1870s, Château Blanchard reminded Benjamin of the expression "castle in the sky." It was the kind of estate that landowners with aspirations once dreamed of building. Only a few, however, could afford such opulence. The exterior was ornate and fascinating, with its intricate pinnacles above the top-floor windows. But as far as Benjamin was concerned, the place was entirely too impractical to live in.

"I'm thinking we should restore the pond. You saw how overrun it is with algae and weeds," Florence said, setting her cup down and casting her eyes over the landscape.

At times Florence seemed overwhelmed by the family legacy. Château Blanchard was too large and its amenities were too few, especially in the winter, when it was impossible to heat. But she loved it in the summer, when children overtook the grounds and dinners under an old magnolia tree at the edge of the pond extended well into the evening.

"One day I'll have the grounds looking like Versailles," Florence said, turning back to Benjamin. "I remember how well my grandfather maintained it."

As the estate's winemaking consultant, Benjamin knew all about the family's history. Florence Blanchard had been born into a family of farmers who had left Algeria during the war of independence in the early 1960s and had ended up in this corner of the Gironde, not far from Château Margaux. This *pied-noir* family had poured all of their resources into their land in the Médoc, and the wines they produced were their pride and joy.

Florence and her brother, Jules, had lost their parents when they were young and had inherited the Blanchard estate from their grandfather. Of the two of them, Florence was the more attached to the fairy-tale château. In her youth, she had spent hours with her grandfather, whose passion for the vine was tireless and unconditional. His cru bourgeois, generated on thirty hectares in the heart of the Listrac appellation, was an elegant and velvety wine approaching the nobility of a Margaux or a Pauillac.

Under her grandfather's tutelage, Florence had developed a love for wine and the land. And as an adult, she had nurtured the vineyards, lush with merlot and cabernet sauvignon rootstock.

"Enough about my plans for the future," Florence said, leaning toward the winemaker. "I have something more pressing on my mind at the moment. Didier seems on edge these days. Should I be worried?"

Didier Morel was the cellar master for Château Blanchard. After finishing his oenological studies, Didier had interned at Château Pichon Longueville Baron and then at Lynch-Bages. Benjamin had met Didier at Lynch-Bages and was so impressed, he advised the Blanchard family to take him on. They hired him on the spot.

The young man had much in common with Benjamin's assistant, Virgile Lanssien. They both had a deeply ingrained passion for rugby, as well as the crafty intelligence of people of the earth. Each had the same diploma signed by the same director of the Institut d'oenologie, the winemaking institute of Bordeaux. These commonalities, however, did not make them allies. Benjamin knew that Virgile was a tad jealous and even reluctant to give his opinion when Florence, Didier, and he presided over the Blanchard blendings. He had concluded that the two were cut from the same cloth, consumed by the same ambitions, and blessed with the same instincts and charm that young women just couldn't resist.

Benjamin smiled. "I wouldn't be concerned. A winemaker's nerves are always on edge during malolactic fermentation. Didier's as vigilant as a lighthouse keeper in a hurricane. His watchfulness is a sign of his commitment."

Florence picked up the silver coffeepot, which was gleaming in the bright sunlight. "Another cup, Benjamin?"

"Gladly," he answered, his gaze once again drawn to the cupola on the slate roof. It seemed pretentious.

Florence followed his gaze. "What do you think of the cupola? I find it rather elegant. It was actually an observation post at one time."

"Is that so?"

"Landowners used cupolas to watch over the vines during harvest. From up there, my grandfather could see as far away as the Garonne and spot any evildoers intent on stealing his grapes. It seems that grape theft was once fairly common."

"Unlike the vines, trust has never thrived in the Médoc," said Benjamin. "The people here are capable of fighting over a single vine stalk for generations. They'd even kill over one."

Florence sipped her coffee. "Something seems to be on your mind, Benjamin."

The winemaker did not respond, mostly because he didn't think he was being overly pensive. Actually, he had arrived early so that he and Florence could have a conversation before her brother and Didier joined them for their tasting. He liked her quick wit, her candor, and her graciousness.

Finally, Benjamin decided to weigh in on the cupolas. "Florence, I don't believe this story about lookouts for the vineyards. In Bordeaux, above the Palais de la Bourse, you see the same cupolas, and as far as I know, there aren't any vineyards around there in danger of being pillaged."

"Benjamin, in the city those cupolas served another purpose altogether. They were for spotting the arrival of merchant ships, which were so vital to the city's economy. Did you know that in the port's heyday there were as many as two thousand ships trading in front of the rostral columns at the Place des Quinconces?"

"Your knowledge impresses me, Florence."

"I do enjoy putting the famous *Cooker Guide* author in his place when I have the chance. After all, your expertise is said to be beyond compare."

"I've never claimed to be infallible," Benjamin answered.

"I should hope not. However, I worry about anyone who believes in ghosts, has no faith in humankind's integrity, and uses artificial sweetener in his coffee."

The Blanchard heiress capped this string of reproaches with a warm smile that spoke volumes about their friendship.

Before the winemaker could respond, he spotted Jules and Didier heading their way.

2

Virgile Lanssien's bachelor pad on the Rue Saint Rémi was one of those small apartments without much character behind old Bordeaux's beautiful eighteenth-century facades. It had a tiny living room with a modest amount of molding, a fireplace with a cracked marble surround, a wood floor, a hallway leading to a cramped bedroom with a window, a bathroom, and a kitchen barely larger than a telephone booth.

The best feature of this home was its balcony. The landlord had described it as a "gorgeous little balcony with a view of the Place de la Bourse and the Fountain of the Three Graces." Actually, it was a merely an opening with a metal barrier in front. From it, Virgile could see a muddy strip of the Garonne River and the plump hips of the muses sculpted long ago.

No matter. Virgile was fine with it. The apartment was neither spacious nor comfortable, but it was two steps from the Allées de Tourny and a stone's throw from the laboratory on the Cours du

Chapeau Rouge. Good thing, too, because he was late. He was supposed to meet Alexandrine de La Palussière—Cooker and Co.'s lab director. She wanted his help because of his ability to discern TCA, or 2,4,6-trichloroanisole, in wine at about two parts per trillion. Not all tasters could pick up cork taint in such small quantities.

Thank God—anything to get out of going to Château Blanchard. He couldn't stand Didier Morel. His boss loved to compare them, but all Virgile could see was that Didier's shoulders were just that much wider than his, his features a tad more chiseled, his legs stronger, and, worse, everything Virgile did, Didier tried to do better. It had started at wine school. Virgile would propose a project about organic farming and the effect on wine production in Bordeaux, and two weeks later Didier would hand in something on biodynamic grape husbandry in Burgundy. Even at the bar, Didier would hit on the same women. It was annoying—like being trailed by a gnat. And now that bloodsucker was hanging around the lab—where Virgile was supposed to have been fifteen minutes ago.

Virgile rummaged through the jeans and underwear strewn all over the floor for something clean to wear. Housekeeping wasn't in his wheelhouse. Sometimes he paid his next-door neighbor to tidy the apartment, but she hadn't been there in a while. She was out of town, visiting her sister in

Mimizan. The place was even grubbier and more cluttered than usual, a dump where a mother cat wouldn't be able to find her kittens.

He tripped on an empty wine bottle, catching himself on the coffee table, where he knocked over a box from the Indian takeout place.

"Dammit."

After brushing his teeth and splashing on some Gentleman by Givenchy, he headed to the kitchen to brew some coffee. Three days of dirty dishes were piled in the sink. He opened the refrigerator, and a rancid odor hit him in the face. His phone buzzed.

It was Alexandrine.

"Don't get your panties in a bunch, Alex. I'm on my way."

There was silence on the line.

"Alex?"

"Is this Mr. Virgile Lanssien?"

"Who's this? What are you doing with Alexandrine's telephone?"

"This is the emergency room at Saint André Hospital. Ms. de La Palussière is here with us. She asked that we call you."

3

"Benjamin! It's good to see you. How's that beautiful wife of yours?" Jules asked.

"Elisabeth's positively giddy. My publisher is whisking us away to Hungary via Vienna."

"Lucky dog. Good thing you could come to see us before you go tasting the king of wines and the wine of kings."

"Yes, that is the reputation of the Tokay wines— ever since the Prince of Transylvania gave a bottle to King Louis XIV, and the king called it *vinum regum, rex vinorum.* I admit I'm looking forward to it."

"Tokay or Tokaji, Mr. Cooker?" Didier asked.

"Good point, young man. Tokay refers to wines from the Tokaj region in Hungary, although for centuries that name had been used for other wines: neighboring Slovakian wines, a pinot gris in Alsace, an Italian grape variety, and even an Australian sweet. Then in 2007, the Eastern European wine region won the right to be the only ones to use that name, no matter how you spell it. The 'i' at the end of Tokaji means "from"

Tokaj, where they make more wines than just the sweet nectar we commonly refer to as Tokay. So, you are right. Tokaji it is."

Didier flashed a grin and ran his hand over a head of curls. Then he added, "How's Margaux?"

"My daughter isn't budging from New York," Benjamin said. It came out sharper than he had intended.

"So you're still keeping her away from the locals like Didier here?" Jules said with a wink.

"Going by the scratches on his forearm, I'd say that's a good thing," Benjamin said, pursing his lips. As much as he liked the boy, neither he nor Virgile were suitable matches for his beloved daughter. They were still busy playing the field.

Didier looked down, then shrugged. "Rough match last night."

Florence cleared her throat. "Why don't we start? Where's Virgile?"

"He won't be joining us," Benjamin said. "A cork-taint problem."

"Too bad," Didier said. Benjamin couldn't tell by his tone if he was disappointed or relieved.

The three men and Florence walked over the grounds to the wine cellar. Benjamin welcomed its coolness. He put on his glasses and took out his notepad.

On a pedestal table covered with an oilcloth, several bottles awaited the verdict of this jury of tasters, just as several other bottles had awaited them the previous year, when, after a gloomy spring and a hot, dry summer, the grapes had been harvested under a copper sun, yielding a perfectly balanced wine blessed by the gods.

What would this tasting bring? Benjamin was eager to find out. His conclusions would make their way into his updated *Cooker Guide*. The guide, five hundred pages long, had become the definitive wine bible, as well as a bestseller, to the great satisfaction of Claude Nithard, his publisher.

Florence filled the wineglasses without spilling a drop. Benjamin plunged his nose into his glass, sniffed, and scribbled in his notebook. He sipped. Silence. Just as he was about to say something, his cell phone vibrated. He frowned and pulled the phone out of his pocket. It was Virgile. "Bad news," the screen read. "Serious! Call me, ASAP."

"Please excuse me," he muttered as he put his glass down and took leave of the Blanchards. He tapped callback and put the phone to his ear.

"Yes, Virgile. More troubles at the lab?"

"No, boss, worse. You've got to come. Someone attacked Alexandrine. She's in bad shape. Her face is a mess. I'm with her in the emergency room at Saint André's."

"I'll be there as soon as I can. Who would do such a thing? To Alexandrine, of all people."

"I don't know, boss. She hasn't told me anything, and I haven't pressed her."

Benjamin ended the call. Hurrying back to the Blanchards, he asked that sample bottles be prepared for him right away.

"There's something I must tend to, and I need to leave. It's an emergency. I'm terribly sorry. I'll share my tasting notes with you later. I promise."

"Nothing serious, I hope," Florence said.

The winemaker mopped his forehead with his linen handkerchief and collected himself. He didn't want to look as frazzled as he felt.

"I'll know better when I get back to Bordeaux. Thank you. I'll be in touch."

Benjamin hurried to his Mercedes convertible and sped away. Fortunately, traffic was light. Saint André Hospital, founded in the fourteenth century, was in the center of town. The buildings, situated around a garden, had managed to retain a certain historical cachet.

Benjamin rushed into the emergency room, and a nurse pointed him to the cubby where Alexandrine was being treated. When he got there, another nurse was helping her into a wheelchair.

"Mr. Cooker," Alexandrine said. Her words were muffled, as she could barely move her swollen lips. Her face was puffy and bruised, her eyes fleeting.

"Don't speak, child. The doctors will take good care of you." The nurse wheeled her away, down the brightly lit hallway.

"Did you see that? Her nose is probably broken, and the bone above her eye looks smashed. Whoever did this had it in for her," Virgile said.

"Has she told you anything yet?"

"No. She just wanted me to tell you not to worry and to go ahead and take that trip to Budapest, as you and Mrs. Cooker had planned."

"I can't do that."

"Listen, boss, it's not every day that your publisher pays for a cruise on the Danube. 'The Blue Danube' and all."

"That, son, would be 'On the Beautiful Blue Danube' or, in the original German, 'An der schönen blauen Donau.'"

"Whatever. I know for a fact that Mrs. Cooker is packed and waiting. Go. Live it up. I'll make sure Alexandrine is okay, and I'll cover the work at the lab."

Benjamin wouldn't leave. They sat in silence for a good hour, but Alexandrine had not yet reappeared.

"Boss, getting her X-rayed will probably take forever, and who knows what they'll need to do after that. You should go. You've got some papers to sign at the office and bags to pack."

"I feel terrible about this, Virgile."

"No worries, boss," Virgile said, mustering a smile. "I got this."

"You'll have your work cut out for you while I'm gone. Keep me posted on Alexandrine."

Benjamin left the emergency room more slowly than he had come in. He said a silent prayer for Alexandrine's recovery and got back in his car to drive to the Cooker & Co. office. If he couldn't be in Bordeaux over the next couple of weeks, at least he could make things a little easier for his assistant.

4

Benjamin had met Claude Nithard many years earlier, before he had even finished his first *Cooker Guide*. Although he was already a leading wine expert, Benjamin didn't consider himself a writer. The publishing-house executive had taken the winemaker under his wing and given him both guidance and support. Since then, the *Cooker Guide* had succeeded well beyond expectation, and the two men had become good friends. Two or three times a year, they would go to Lutétia in Paris and share an epicurean feast. Three saints would invariably join them—Saint Julien, Saint Estèphe, and Saint Émilion. They would spend a few hours in heaven and leave the restaurant in a serene state of communion.

This year, Claude had called Benjamin a few hours before the newest edition of the *Cooker Guide* was scheduled to go to press. He wanted to do something more spectacular than going to the Lutétia, as he was celebrating not only the updated *Cooker Guide*, but also a milestone birthday.

Claude asked Benjamin and Elisabeth to join his girlfriend and him on a Danube River cruise.

"We'll visit the Tokaji winemaking region," he had told Benjamin. "It was my girlfriend's idea. She's already making the arrangements with my secretary. The publishing house will treat, of course."

A romantic cruise on the Danube: as soon as Claude made the offer, Benjamin was envisioning himself gliding through the waters, his glass in hand and his preferred cigar between his lips. They'd board in Vienna and cruise to Budapest, where they'd take in the city's smoky cafés, Turkish baths, quaint hotels, and baroque character. And finally they'd get on the legendary Bartók Béla and travel by rail to Bald Mountain, which, ironically, was covered with forests and vines.

Claude claimed to know little about Hungary, except for having played an interminable game of chess in the well-known Széchenji baths of Budapest. The winemaker enthusiastically offered to be the ad hoc guide, knowing, as he did, all about the liquid gold that trickled down the languid slopes of Mount Tokaj.

That had been several weeks earlier—before someone smashed in Alexandrine's face. Although he knew Virgile would take good care of her and Cooker & Co., he didn't feel right about leaving.

"What's wrong, darling?" Elisabeth asked as they headed to the airport.

Benjamin harrumphed.

"You're such a worrywart. I talked to Alexandrine. She's shook up, but she insisted that you not concern yourself. Virgile's with her."

Elisabeth leaned over and kissed him on the cheek.

"Think of what awaits us," she said. "The proud Buda, the boisterous Pest, the stalls of paprika, the Herend porcelain, the sweets at the Gerbeaud café. How long has it been, sweetheart, since we've had a getaway like this?"

Benjamin relaxed a little and cleared his throat. "I see we even got a new set of luggage. Was that really necessary?"

"Oh, don't be a curmudgeon. Wait until you see the clothes I bought. There's a little lacy thing that I think you'll especially like."

5

As soon as they arrived at the Hotel Sacher in Vienna, Benjamin called Alexandrine, but she didn't answer her phone. He left a quick message telling her he was thinking of her. Then he called Virgile.

"So?"

"She'll be in the hospital for a few days, boss, and won't be able to work for more than a month."

"What's the extent of the damage?"

"The attack was brutal. Her brow's fractured. Her nasal septum's broken, and her optic nerve may be injured. The doctors think she might need reconstructive surgery."

Benjamin pictured her delicate and perfectly shaped nose and grimaced.

"Has she talked to the police?"

"Yep. She gave them a short description of the man. Late forties, square face, short hair, crooked teeth. That's all. She said he seemed to have it in for her. He called her names and hit her hard several times. Then he grabbed her purse and ran off."

"Odd."

"What's that, boss?"

"That's a lot of violence for a purse snatching. Where did it take place?"

"In the Allées des Tourny parking garage."

"It's a busy place. There must be cameras. Check with the police and make sure they're looking into it."

"Um, boss, do you think the police will want me to tell them how to do their job?"

"Call Inspector Barbaroux. He owes me one."

"Doesn't he work homicide? This is just a mugging."

"Just a mugging?" Benjamin could feel his blood pressure rising. "How can you say that? This is Alexandrine we're talking about!"

Benjamin ended the call without saying good-bye. He took a few deep breaths, straightened his jacket, and joined Elisabeth in the lobby.

6

Benjamin found Elisabeth in the grand salon. Her simple beige dress accentuated her slender frame and classic good looks, and she looked effortlessly chic in her go-with-everything trench coat, Hermès scarf, and buckled low-heeled pumps. Elisabeth smiled and took his arm as he cast his eyes over the luxurious banquettes and marble pedestal tables laden with sweets. Clearly, the sin of gluttony was a virtue here.

"You did promise there'd be no mention of the word 'diet,' right?" Benjamin whispered as they sat down at their table.

"It *is* hard to resist a Sachertorte with all that decadent chocolate, isn't it?"

"Especially with a dollop of whipped cream. Turning it down would be sacrilege."

Elisabeth looked him in the eye with a gaze that caused Benjamin's heart to skip a beat.

"Okay, no diet, but only if you keep your part of the deal." She leaned over and nuzzled his neck.

Benjamin Cooker, the staid half-English Frenchman, felt himself blush like a schoolboy.

He cleared his throat and looked up when he heard his name called. Claude Nithard, wearing a perfectly tailored jacket, narrow trousers, and pointed leather shoes, was waving and walking toward them with a ravishing brunette.

"Let me introduce Consuela Chavez."

The Cookers stood up to greet Claude and Consuela with the traditional French cheek kisses. Despite a marked difference in age, the Nithard-Chavez couple seemed compatible. They were holding hands, and Consuela was giggling. Benjamin wondered where she was from—perhaps from Central or South America? She was beautiful, indeed. And one who seemed to crave attention. Benjamin hadn't missed the smoky eye makeup and the way she swayed as they were walking to the table.

"I hope we haven't kept you waiting," Claude said.

"We had just enough time to decide that our first adventure would be Sachertorte." Benjamin started to pull out a chair for Consuela, but Claude hastened to do it himself, giving his lover an intimate look as she sat down. Benjamin wrinkled his nose. Their bond smelled of fresh paint.

"Will that be four servings?" Benjamin asked, sitting down.

Consuela declined. "I'll have a Viennese coffee, without too much whipped cream, please."

"Oh, but you must try the Sachertorte," Claude pressed, explaining that the confection was a specialty of the grandest hotel in Vienna. Generations of Austrians had been willing to sell their souls for just a taste. Such grand words were a bit too much, even for Claude.

Still, the woman refused, giving her lover a pouty look with her own version of creative drama.

Elisabeth glanced at Benjamin, and he knew she was going to roll her eyes. He hastened to make some conversation.

"Did you know that the pastry chefs who make the Sachertorte here go through more than a million eggs every year, plus eighty tons of sugar, seventy-five tons of chocolate, thirty-seven tons of apricot jam, twenty-five tons of butter, and no less than thirty tons of flour?"

Elisabeth raised her hand to quiet her husband. "Stop showing off, Benjamin. I love chocolate cake as much as anyone else, but all that tonnage is making me queasy."

"Not me," Claude said, motioning to the waiter. "Benjamin, you and Elisabeth should write a cookbook for us. I don't know why I didn't think of it sooner. You have the perfect name: Cooker. I can see the title now: *Cooking with the Cookers*. With the dishes Elisabeth turns out and your wine pairings, we'd have the makings of a bestseller, I tell you."

"Claude, you were the one who said no work on this trip," Benjamin answered. "And now you're trying to convince me to write another book? As if there weren't mountains of cookbooks already. And who buys them anymore? Margaux says that everyone gets recipes off the Internet these days."

Across from him, Consuela was fingering the silverware and giving him a provocative look. The winemaker caught himself feeling intrigued. Elisabeth's quick jab under the table stopped him. He gave his wife a sheepish look and was grateful when their sweets arrived. He picked up his spoon and dived in.

"Did you know that there's a fascinating story behind this cake?" the winemaker asked.

"Really?" It was Consuela.

"Yes," Benjamin said, wiping his mouth with his napkin, stamped with the hotel's coat of arms. "It was at the beginning of the nineteenth century. Prince Klemens Wenzel von Metternich ordered his bakers to create a unique dessert for some dignitaries he wanted to impress. 'Do not disappoint or shame me,' the prince told the kitchen staff. Unfortunately, the head pastry chef was bedridden, and it fell on his sixteen-year-old apprentice, Franz Sacher, to take up the challenge and prepare an amazing chocolate cake. You can imagine how his knees were shaking when he presented the cake. But as it turned out, his creation delighted both the prince and his guests. It wasn't long before the cake became renowned throughout

Vienna. And today, as you can see, people come from all over to order this very confection."

"It's good," Elisabeth said, putting down her spoon. "Very good, even. But legendary? I don't know."

Benjamin smiled at his wife. She was a discerning woman. One of the many qualities he loved about her.

"Things aren't always what they seem," he said. "Perhaps the legend doesn't come from the actual cake, but from the story surrounding it. Franz's son Edouard carried on the family tradition and perfected the cake while working for the competition—the Demel Bakery. He did well enough to open his own hotel—the Sacher Hotel: But it wound up going bankrupt, and Edouard's son returned to Demel. By 1938, however, the Sacher Hotel was up and running again under different ownership. It began making the cake too. The rivalry was on, eventually leading to litigation. Each side laid claim to the original Sachertorte."

"Sounds like a classic copyright dispute," Claude said. "Who won?"

"The tussle lasted for years. The two sides set in motion the entire Austrian legal machine, whose rulings were challenged one by one. Pastry chefs from all over the world were asked to give their expert testimony. Finally, in 1965, the Vienna Supreme Court ruled in favor of the Hotel Sacher, affirming it as owner of the original Sachertorte.

The recipe was placed in the establishment's vault, where it remains to this day."

Benjamin took his fork and poked at the confection. "The two cakes are a bit different. Here it's filled with apricot jam, while at Demel's it's covered with a warm layer of apricot marmalade and frosted with chocolate. If we have time before boarding the ship to Budapest tomorrow, we can visit Demel's."

"I don't know, Benjamin," Elisabeth said. "That's cutting it a bit close."

"So what about the rest of today?" Claude said, finishing his cake. "Would you care to join Consuela and me? We're thinking of checking out the Gustav Klimt paintings at the Schönbrunn Palace."

Benjamin wasn't surprised, considering the erotic nature of Klimt's work. Elisabeth gave him a don't-you-dare glare. He smiled at Claude and said they had their own plans. The Cookers accompanied the publisher and his companion to their cab and said good-bye.

"So, my love, if not Klimt, then what?"

"The Hofburg Palace?"

The former imperial palace was grand, but Benjamin was hoping to see the house where Mozart had composed the *Coronation Mass*.

"All right. I'm too thrilled to be in Vienna to argue," Elisabeth said, smiling and taking her husband's arm. "Let's go see Wolfgang's place."

7

Back at the hotel, Benjamin called Virgile.

"Boss, something's off with Alexandrine's story. The police checked the surveillance cameras, and they didn't pick up anything. There weren't any traces of blood in the garage, either. The cops came to see Alexandrine again. I was there. They asked the same question you did: why would someone attack her so brutally just to take her purse and run off. They think she may know the attacker—and they were tough on her about it."

"Well, what did she say?"

"Nothing. She was a real clam. She said she passed out after the guy started beating her and barely remembers how she got to the hospital when she came to. A blessing, if you ask me. She's still having a hard time thinking straight."

"What do you think?"

"I think is it's odd that I'm the only one with her at the hospital. Doesn't she have family, boss? Why did she call me?"

Benjamin knew the Palussières were an old family from the Gironde that, apart from some vines and a neo-Gothic château in the haut Médoc, had made its fortune in the slave trade rather than wine. Of course, Alexandrine's ancestors had invented a more glorious past involving the sale of spices on Bordeaux's Cours de la Martinique, as well as a lucrative brokerage business on the Cours de l'Intendance, when Bordeaux wines were shipped all over the world and *négociants* fixed the prices on behalf of the owners of grand cru estates.

These days, the family drew most of its profits from real-estate holdings. Rumor had it that they owned a private mansion on the Rue du Palais Gallien in downtown Bordeaux, two single-story houses called *échoppes* in the upscale suburb of Caudéran, an old monastery property in the town of Latresne, and a waterfront villa on the Arcachon Bay, at the tip of Cap Ferret.

It didn't matter how much money the family had or where it came from. None of it was Alexandrine's. They'd given her an apartment—it wouldn't do to have her homeless—and then cut her off. She was on her own.

"Virgile, her lifestyle choices alienated her family."

"That's so provincial, boss. Hardly anybody thinks that way anymore. And even if they disagreed with her so-called lifestyle choices, you'd think they'd come to see her in the hospital. How could parents abandon their daughter this way?"

"Her parents haven't spoken to her for years, not since she came out. They might not even know that she was attacked. She called you because we're her family now. Do we know anything else?"

"The investigator asked if she received any threats or got any suspicious phone calls in the weeks leading up to the attack."

"Well, did she?"

"She insisted that she didn't."

There was a moment of silence on the phone as Benjamin watched Elisabeth come out of the hotel bathroom in an off-the-shoulder black evening dress and the sexiest spike heels he had ever seen. They had red soles and were nearly see-through. How much had they set him back? He didn't care.

"Boss?"

"Um, yes. Anything in the papers?"

"No, I'm doing my best to keep it low-profile. Cooker & Co. doesn't need this kind of publicity."

"You're right, but our priority is Alexandrine. We need to protect her privacy and take care of her. Thank you, son, for staying by her side."

"No problem, boss. I gave her flowers and said they were from all of us, and yesterday I came with some *cannelés* from the Baillardran bakery. She loves them, especially when the crust is caramelized just right around the custard center."

"Is the work piling up in the lab?"

"Nothing I can't handle."

"If you need to, call in Didier Morel to help you out."

There was another silence. This time from Virgile.

Elisabeth had finished her makeup and looked ravishing in her usual understated way. How could any other woman look more beautiful in this luxurious room, with its crystal chandelier and view of the Vienna State Opera House?

"Virgile, let me share a bit of sage advice: 'Keep your friends close, and your enemies closer.'"

"You and your quotes. Well, I know that one. It's from Sun Zi's *The Art of War*. I heard it on the radio."

"Wrong, my boy. It was Michael Corleone who said that."

"Who?"

"*The Godfather, Part II*."

"You're pulling my leg."

"No. It *is* frequently misattributed to Sun Zi. I'll give you that. Now, I'm off to the opera."

8

The two couples had arranged to meet at eight that evening at the opera house, just across the street from the hotel, for a performance of Mussorgsky's *Night on Bald Mountain*. The casting promised to be brilliant.

The performance, however, failed to deliver. Elisabeth did a poor job of hiding her yawns, and even though Benjamin enjoyed the symphony, the orchestration wasn't as magical as it was in the movie *Fantasia*, which he had seen as a child.

Only Consuela had risen to her feet and burst into applause. Claude, joining her in the standing ovation, beamed at his darling, thrilled that he had given her an evening to remember. Benjamin and Elisabeth exchanged a look.

Afterward, at Walter Bauer, a tiny restaurant on a narrow street in Old Vienna, the two couples sat next to a dark wood-paneled wall and admired the vaulted ceilings.

"Claude, you surprise me. I would have thought the two-Michelin-star Steirereck was more to your taste," Benjamin said.

"I didn't want you to get too distracted by the thirty-five thousand bottles they have in their wine cellar. Besides, I consulted with Elisabeth."

Elisabeth smiled. "Benjamin, you'll like this one. It's unpretentious. It has a Michelin star, and the owner has mentored some of Austria's finest chefs. It's a good fit."

They ordered a mix of traditional dishes, served with flair, and enjoyed a lush aged Blaufränkisch, one of Austria's champion red wines.

Claude swirled and sipped. "It's quite subtle."

"Note the blackberries and citrus-like spice," Benjamin said.

Elisabeth studied the robe and aromas. After a few moments, she tasted the wine and swished it in her mouth, as Benjamin had taught her. She grinned when she put the glass down. "Now, that's what I call a burst of tannins midpalate."

Consuela didn't contribute to the discussion. She was drinking water. An uncomfortable silence fell on the group.

Claude shifted in his seat. "Why is it, Benjamin, that I've never heard anything about Austrian wines before?"

"Because of scandal, my friend. In the nineteen eighties, some Austrian winemakers were lacing their wines with diethylene glycol—or antifreeze,

33

if you prefer. They did it to make late-harvest wines seem more full-bodied and sweeter."

Elisabeth and Claude frowned and stopped sipping.

"Don't worry. They were caught. But the Austrian wine industry collapsed and needed well over a decade to recover—with the help of stricter laws."

Elisabeth turned to Consuela. "Do try the wine."

Consuela pursed her lips and batted her eyelashes.

"Oh, why not?" the woman said. "It is vacation."

A glass of wine loosened her up a bit, and Consuela started talking about herself. She mentioned Caracas and Buenos Aires and hinted at a lifestyle strewn with travels and grueling tours— she was a dancer. Benjamin listened intently, but much of her past remained a mystery. He looked to Claude, hoping their host would fill them in, but the man remained tight-lipped.

"Were you born in Buenos Aires?" Elisabeth asked.

"No, in La Plata," Consuela said. "It's not far from there."

"My husband often goes to Mendoza to make wine for the Bordeaux producers who have vineyards in Argentina, but he has always refused to take me along."

"Elisabeth, how can you say that?" Benjamin said, pretending to be offended.

"Yes, of course, you've promised that we'll go someday. But even though you're still an English gentleman at heart, thanks to your father, you've picked up some less-than-desirable Gascon traits: when you throw out an invitation, my dear, you never specify the month or even the year."

Claude came to his friend's defense. "Why is it that significant others always want to tag along on work trips? No matter how exotic the destination, there's never enough time for leisure or sightseeing."

Elisabeth laughed. "Don't take me for a fool, Claude. We all know that some men refuse their wives what they gladly give their mistresses—and I'm not talking about you, Benjamin. What do you think, Consuela?"

"I have nothing to complain about. I am the wife of no man, just the mistress of many. And all my lovers have satisfied me in one way or another…"

Benjamin saw the light go out in Claude's eyes. Now it was all out in the open. Claude was just the latest in the Latina's succession of lovers. Although Benjamin was repelled by the thought of going to bed with a woman who had taken dozens of lovers, he could understand that this might make her even more desirable to Claude, a man who needed to prove that he was the best.

"Claude is my latest faux pas," she said with a laugh loud enough to make heads turn.

Benjamin looked at his three companions. Consuela was wearing a form-fitting dress that revealed her deliciously tanned shoulders and arms. This woman with emerald-green eyes and sun-kissed skin knew how to draw men to her. But as gorgeous as she was, she was acting like no more than a gypsy fortune-teller—a card reader plotting out her destiny. Benjamin suddenly felt sorry for his friend Claude, who should have known better.

"That calls for Champagne," Claude said.

"Dom Pérignon," Consuela chimed in.

The server delivered the bottle, uncorked it, and poured four glasses. Benjamin raised his. "To Champagne. Like Coco Chanel, one should drink Champagne on only two occasions: when in love and when not in love."

Elisabeth bit her lip to suppress a smile.

Chuckling, Claude patted Consuela's knee, and she leaned over and whispered something in his ear.

Claude answered in Spanish, and the beautiful foreigner laughed even louder. He was staring at the small mole on her bosom.

9

Before heading to the port the next morning, Benjamin insisted that they get up early and have a Viennese breakfast of soft-boiled eggs, rolls, and coffee under the arched ceiling of the Café Central. Claude sent Benjamin a text message at the last minute saying they wouldn't be able to make it, so the two couples met up at the pier.

"Turbulent, wise and great." Hungarian writer Attila József's line in a poem about the Danube came to Benjamin as he waited there with Elisabeth, Claude, and Consuela. The Danube wasn't quite as grand in Vienna as it was in Budapest.

Benjamin lit his robusto while Elisabeth and Consuela fussed with their luggage. Claude was on his phone, settling urgent matters at the publishing house. The race was on for literary prizes, and Claude needed to advance his pawns in order to persuade the jury. It would take some lobbying, as well as a fair amount of circuitous maneuvering. But he excelled in both.

Claude pretended to be modest. In fact, he was envied by his colleagues, feared by his associates, hated by some members of the press, and praised by others. He was an integral member of all the inner circles that counted, and every year he pulled off one publishing coup after another.

Claude was also a voracious reader and an indefatigable worker. He was erudite, refined, and curious about everything. In these respects, he and Benjamin were very similar. Their long-standing friendship was based largely on their shared affinities, which were just as important as the success of the *Cooker Guide*. The two men celebrated their bonds with glasses of vintage Chasse-Spleen and amber Armagnac, along with Montecristos and Épicure No. 2 cigars. And with unbridled imagination, they philosophized. The cruise on the Danube promised moments of charm and tranquility.

Claude ended his call just as they were boarding the ship. Looking preoccupied, he started to put his arm around Consuela. But she stepped in front of him and sashayed past a group of young crewmembers in white shirts. They all stopped and stared, which made Elisabeth give Benjamin another one of her "did you see that" looks. Embarrassed for his friend, Benjamin ignored it and handed a five-euro note to the man taking charge of their bags.

The Danube was silty, and the sky was ashen. This wasn't the way Benjamin had envisioned leaving Vienna. He watched the women head off to their cabins and turned to his friend.

A siren blared at the rear of the boat, and suddenly the dock was far away. Minutes later, the Ferris wheel in the amusement park was no more than a pinwheel lost in the distance, and the spire of the Gothic Maria am Gestade church was trying in vain to pierce the black clouds hovering over the Austrian capital. Vienna was dissolving in the morning light. Beyond the hills, a thunderstorm was brewing. Beneath them, the wind was rippling the waters of the Danube and spraying gray foam onto its miry banks.

At the prow, Claude borrowed Benjamin's lighter to rekindle his Havana. The two men puffed and silently took in the landscape. Flashes of lightning, followed by heavy drops of rain, soon dissuaded them from playing lookout any longer. The thunderstorm was quickly rolling toward the Danube. A second later, lightning struck a clump of poplars next to the river.

Claude and Benjamin retreated to the sitting room.

"Benjamin, this cruise line may not have sleek longships, but it does have charm and authenticity. I told Consuela it was just your style."

And because the publishing house was picking up the tab, the lower cost had most likely suited him, Benjamin thought. The sitting room, with its leatherette armchairs, faded posters, and Art

Deco–inspired bar wasn't exactly charming, but he still liked the unpretentious feel of the ship.

Most of the passengers seemed to have taken refuge inside. They weren't numerous: a mismatched couple probably from the United States; three Asian tourists; some corpulent men who looked Russian; two red-haired girls, freckled and as tall as poplars; a bearded man, English or Scottish, clutching a sketchbook; an old woman in a wheelchair accompanied by a dour attendant; two tanned men wearing similar expensive watches and designer shirts; and finally a willowy young woman with straight blond hair that fell to her shoulders. She was wearing a turtleneck and a long cape, reminding Benjamin of Michèle Morgan in *La Symphonie Pastorale*, which he had seen several years earlier in a film retrospective.

"Have I ever told you, Claude, that my one regret to date is never having experienced an ocean crossing from Southampton to New York?"

"Does that stem from some nostalgia for old-style luxury?"

"Claude, it is so much more. 'Man cannot discover new oceans unless he has the courage to lose sight of the shore.'"

"André Gide," Claude responded. "A man who fearlessly explored the shores of his own nature."

Benjamin nodded. This man of letters was as facile with quotes as he was. "Let's explore this ship, my friend," he said, taking Claude's elbow. "And I think we should start at the bar."

In anticipation of the vineyards in the Eger region, which had been making wine since the thirteenth century, Benjamin proposed ordering two glasses of Egri Bikavér. This most famous of Hungarian wines was a deep crimson, true to its name, bull's blood.

Benjamin was hoping it would lift their spirits. Claude seemed disturbed by his phone call. Benjamin, meanwhile, couldn't shake his worries about Alexandrine. The two friends remained mostly silent as they sipped their drinks and watched the landscape pass by, commenting only now and then on the fauna and flora, some onion-shaped domes, a pair of gray herons, a migratory bird rising from a reedy marsh, and the black poplars. Nothing terribly exotic. Just the last stretch before they reached the East.

The beautiful Consuela, in a clingy black dress slit to her satiny thigh, interrupted the men's somber musings. Claude slipped his arm around her waist. Without a word, the woman picked up Claude's glass and sipped his bull's blood. No sooner had she tasted it than she made a face and spit it back in the glass.

"How do you drink this stuff, Claude? Some Champagne! Nothing but Champagne!" she ordered the bartender, who was already undressing her with his eyes.

10

Virgile said a few words to the duty nurse. Her cheeks turned red, and he flashed one of his grins before heading to Alexandrine's room. He was bearing *praslines* from Blaye. Benjamin had told him all about this caramel-coated almond delicacy during a walk through the fortified town. It was named after a certain Count of Plessis-Praslin, a seventeenth-century military man with a delicate stomach. Virgile, however, was more interested in the crunchy texture and mildly toasted flavor of the *prasline* than its history.

Alexandrine actually smiled at the sight of him, which was an improvement. One wall in the room had been painted a solid green, and she had a view out the window—not of the fountain in the main courtyard though.

He sat down in the single chair next to the bed. He told her about the tests they were running in the lab and the calls they were getting. Then he filled her in on Benjamin's latest adventures.

"He wants me to call in Didier Morel to help out."

Alexandrine turned and looked out the window. They sat in silence a bit.

"I don't mean to pry, Alexandrine, but I've been curious about something. I thought you had a girlfriend, but I haven't seen her at the hospital."

"Chloé? We had a fight, the week before I was…"

"You were living together, weren't you?"

"Not really. It depended on our moods. She was an insanely jealous woman."

"Are you saying that you were unfaithful?"

"You're a fine one to talk! You, the unrepentant womanizer, calling me promiscuous? I'd be careful if I were you."

"That's not what I mean, Alex. Believe me. It's just that I don't understand your Chloé. If she really loved you, she'd be at your side at the hospital. I don't care how mad she was. She would have put her anger aside and been with you. Unless she was the one who attacked you."

"Just forget about Chloé. Get it? It's over! Finished. And she had nothing to do with what happened."

"So she's not the one who beat your face in? Maybe you just don't want to report her to the police. People in love do stupid things."

"Do you really believe what you're saying?"

"Yup, and I'm not the only one. The cops don't believe you're telling the whole story either. Alex, you need to put your cards on the table."

"So, according to you, I'm nothing but a filthy liar."

43

"Alex, you are a desirable, sweet, intelligent, and capable woman. As far as Cooker & Co. is concerned, you're indispensable. Your personal life concerns only you. What I'm saying is that you need to be honest about this. That's all."

Alexandrine turned away. Virgile stayed for a while, but she closed her eyes and soon fell asleep.

Virgile wandered down the hall to find the coffee machine. Before leaving the floor, he turned back to wave good-bye to the duty nurse, and he could have sworn that he saw Didier Morel, with the curly dark hair and muscular shoulders, making her giggle.

11

A great crested grebe dived from the sky and vanished in the Danube waters. Just as quickly, it resurfaced with a small fish in its beak. Benjamin and Claude, who couldn't summon the concentration to focus on the manuscript he was reading, silently watched the predator's attack—that is, when he wasn't staring at the predators interested in Consuela.

Consuela, stretched out on a white canvas deck chair, her eyes half-closed, was offering her body to the Hungarian sun. With a delicate maneuver and a mischievous twinkle in her eye, she carefully lowered the straps of her jersey dress and gently pulled the skirt above her knees. It looked like she had done it not for Claude, but for the crewmembers in white shirts who kept trying to attract her attention with whistles and comments Benjamin couldn't understand.

Elisabeth, who had slathered on the sunscreen and found a chair under an umbrella, was dressed modestly in a loose top, capri pants, and espadrilles.

She looked lovingly at Benjamin, who, like Claude, was struggling to read a book.

"Benjamin, walk with me," she said, setting down her crossword puzzle.

Benjamin got up and tossed the paperback on the deck chair.

Elisabeth took his arm. "What were you trying to read?"

"It's a gift from Claude, although who knows why he gave it to me. It's a forensic science thriller with cadavers turning up in every nook and cranny of the Paris Natural History Museum. The plot is convoluted and saturated with anatomical details. It's truly not to my liking."

"Perhaps he'd like you to write a thriller next, after the cookbook."

"Ha. Give me a classic any day, or some underappreciated gem written by a gifted writer."

"I've caught you reading nonfiction before."

"History, mostly."

"Darling, I suspect that it's your distracted mind, not the book, that's at fault here."

Elisabeth knew him too well. The vacation, the taste of freedom as he headed toward the Black Sea, the soothing landscape unfolding before his eyes— none of this could wrest him from his thoughts.

They stopped behind the bearded artist, who was sketching the boat's crew. After a few minutes, they walked on.

"You're still back in Bordeaux, picturing yourself in the vines and consumed with the blendings."

"You're right, my dear. I'm worried about Alexandrine. Who would do that to her? And what really happened? She knows more than she's saying."

"Why don't you just ask her?"

"It wouldn't be right. I'm her employer, and there's a fine line I have to respect."

"She's in good hands with Virgile. He'll charm the information out of her—when she's ready."

"That boy has too much charm, if you ask me. I'm glad he's spending time with Alexandrine, but I'm worried about the lab. Virgile needs to be there too. The tests are piling up. This is the worst possible time to be on vacation."

"Stop kicking yourself. Virgile is handling everything—and quite capably, I'm sure. Meanwhile, remember that you are supposed to be an easygoing disciple of Epicurus who forgets his worries. The sky is blue, the glass is full, and the pleasures of the flesh close at hand, so unless you're suggesting my company isn't excellent, drop the glum face."

Benjamin felt the tension drain out of him as he watched the graceful gesture she used to move the hair out of her eyes. There was something of a younger Charlotte Rampling about Elisabeth. Her blue eyes, even without makeup, were piercing and alluring. He admired the nonchalant and discreet way she had taken it upon herself to make him feel better. She was his rock.

"You and Claude make quite a couple. We're floating past all this peaceful Hungarian landscape, and he's got his very affectionate Consuela to keep him warm at night, yet he's distracted too."

They both looked over at Claude. A dark cloud seemed to hang over his face. Then he smiled at them and ran his fingers through his silver hair as if to hide his unspoken sadness.

"You know that his divorce from Pilar was long and painful. I don't think he feels capable of happiness yet."

Benjamin and Elisabeth both swung around at the sound of an argument. With lightning reflexes, the artist was grabbing his sketchpad back from a teenager who seemed intent on stealing it. The artist was yelling and waving his fist as the kid ran off before anyone got a good look at him.

12

When Virgile showed up at Cooker & Co., he found Jacqueline, the office manager, laughing and Didier Morel half sitting on her desk, his hands clasped and a perfect smile on his face.

Virgile shot Jacqueline a questioning look, and then, feeling harried and annoyed, he peered around the office, with its Second Empire feel and jumble of modern devices. His eyes landed on his own desk. He was about to ask if any reports from the lab had come in when Didier strode over to shake his hand.

"Virgile, my friend! It's good to see you. We missed you at the Blanchard tasting. I was glad to see Benjamin again."

"Didier has come in to help us," Jacqueline said. "Mr. Cooker called to tell me this morning."

Now Virgile was really irritated. He had already charged Emmanuel Ladevèze, a lab assistant whom Alexandrine had recruited the previous year, with overseeing the analyses at the Rue Chapeau Rouge laboratory.

49

"I heard what happened to Alexandrine," Didier said. "It's terrible."

Virgile hated how Didier used first names so casually. He'd seen Alexandrine talking with him on several occasions at the lab—and even arguing, now that he thought about it—but still.

"Yes, Ms. de la Palussière will be away for a while, but we've got the lab under control."

Now Jacqueline was looking at Virgile over the top of her glasses, as if she wondered whether he truly understood how fortunate they were to have Didier's help. He sighed. He didn't want to be anywhere near Didier, but this was what the boss wanted.

"It's true, with the mildew attacks throughout the southwest, we've got a lot on our plates," Virgile finally said. "We'll have to get out to each grower and adjust the treatments."

"No sweat. I'm happy to help. We'll need to verify the extent of the damage, the stage of vine growth, and the temperature variations."

"Of course," Virgile said. He knew all that. Didier was being so patronizing. Virgile would have to keep two steps ahead of him to hold this man in check. Some help this was!

13

Unable to sleep that night, Benjamin got up, threw on his sweater, and went up to the deck with thoughts of lighting a cigar. The boat was docked in Bratislava, and the city lights obscured any view of the night sky. Still, the air was refreshingly cool, and Benjamin allowed himself to be lulled by the gentle swaying of the ship.

Leaning against the railing, two crewmembers, apparently just off duty, were smoking cigarettes and making jokes. Were they drunk? Benjamin gave them a polite smile and quietly headed toward the prow, where he spotted Claude's silhouette and approached without saying a word.

"You couldn't sleep either?" Claude said without turning around.

Benjamin took a Montecristo from his cigar case and offered one to Claude. His friend demurred.

"Not tonight, Benjamin."

"You're right. It's hard to smoke when you've got a lump in your throat," the winemaker said.

Claude didn't respond. The crewmembers' laughter was getting louder, but he didn't seem to notice.

"Consuela?" Benjamin finally asked.

"Yes, I know what you're going to say. She's much too young for me." Claude turned toward his friend. "She's a terrific lover, you know."

"I wouldn't doubt that for a minute," Benjamin said, puffing his cigar to keep it lit.

"I know she'll leave me one day. Maybe it would be better to leave her before she ends it with me."

"Carpe diem, Claude. Carpe diem."

Claude smiled and patted Benjamin's back.

"I'm glad you came, Benjamin. You really are a good friend."

The two men spoke awhile and then went to join the lively crewmembers, who, as it turned out, were Hungarians.

The older one—Viktor—held up the keys to the bar and lifted an invisible bottle to his mouth with a grin that revealed a missing lower tooth. Benjamin and Claude shrugged and accepted the invitation.

Viktor tossed the keys to the younger man, Attila, who went off to fetch some beers, which the four men downed under the stars. Attila suggested that they take in a few of the shady bars in Budapest, where the girls weren't shy, as long as the customer had a fat wallet.

Benjamin declined, but Claude didn't say anything. Viktor, the more resourceful of the two freshwater swabs, scribbled his cell phone number on a scrap of newspaper.

"Let me know if you're looking for a good time," Viktor seemed to be saying, handing the phone number to Claude. The tipsy crewmember then made a show of licking his middle finger, running it under his half-unbuttoned shirt, and rubbing his nipple like a performer in a peep show.

Benjamin was repelled. He flicked his spent cigar into the black waters of the Danube.

The Hungarians said "*joestét*." Benjamin and Claude said "good night" in return.

Claude waited until they were out of sight before crumpling the slip of paper and tossing it into the river. The two Frenchmen staggered back to their cabins.

14

It was almost noon when the Hungarian capital rose above the calm waters of the Danube. Benjamin hardly recognized the city. His last visit to Hungary had been decades earlier, when he had come with a group of Aquitaine investors who wanted to buy forty hectares in the Tokaj wine region. Communist rule had just ended, and state-owned farms were being privatized. Benjamin and his clients had flown in, and the winemaker still remembered the acrid yellow smoke hovering over Budapest. At the time, Csepel Island was a forest of factory chimneys.

On the ship's deck, all eyes were on Gellért Hill. On the left bank, Pest languidly revealed itself. It was the threshold of the fertile Hungarian plains. On the opposite bank, stately old buildings lined the steep hills of Buda. The rococo-style homes, painted yellow and ocher, seemed to be basking in the sunlight.

Benjamin had just talked to Virgile, who was grumbling about his executive decision to bring in Didier Morel.

"How's Alexandrine?" Elisabeth asked.

"Virgile says she's still in the hospital. He goes every day and says the nurses think they're a couple."

"Are they? I thought he was still sweet on Margaux."

Benjamin stiffened and looked away.

Consuela joined them and began sharing information gleaned from the guidebooks.

Cigar in hand, Benjamin wandered off and found Claude, who was taking in the spires, belfries, rounded roofs, and onion domes. At times like this, Benjamin regretted giving up art. He would have enjoyed rendering the scenery. But his days as a student artist were long gone, and he had chosen an altogether different journey. He looked at his friend, relit his cigar, and silently watched the landscape pass by.

When the landing came into view, the passengers started moving about. His moleskin sketchbook in hand, the bearded Scotsman—or Englishman—was still busy drawing the contours of Buda and seemed indifferent to the activity all around him. The crewmembers had donned their caps. Their smiles were sincere, and their bright eyes augured a promising stay. Benjamin recognized Viktor. He gave him a firm handshake, as did Claude. Consuela flashed the Hungarian a killer smile before walking down the gangway.

On the dock, in a uniform a bit too large for him, a young man was brandishing a sign that read "Astoria Hotel." Consuela quickly waved to him.

The chauffeur merely nodded and took their bags with no hint of subservience. He invited Benjamin to take a seat in the front with him but didn't bother to smile.

The Astoria was the legendary palace of Budapest. In its salon, the country's first democratic government was formed in 1918, after the collapse of the Austro-Hungarian Empire. A century later, nothing seemed to have changed, other than the computer screens at the reception desk. The spirit of the early twentieth century still reigned, with its exquisite elegance, stucco, copper, and mahogany woodwork.

"I would have preferred the Danubius Hotel Gellért," Claude said.

"It is an art nouveau jewel, isn't it," Benjamin answered. "I stayed there the last time I was here."

"Unfortunately, it was fully booked."

In the backseat, Consuela turned to Claude. "How are we ever going to see everything?"

"We'll have time enough," Claude countered. "We can take in the Erdody Palace, the royal Buda Castle, the Church of Saint Anne, and maybe Grassalkovich Palace in one day."

But he failed to satisfy his lover. "Claude, it's impossible to do everything you said. I want to visit the baths. And Mrs. Cooker, too. Right?"

Claude leaned forward and tapped Benjamin's shoulder. "We'll do whatever you ladies wish, won't we, Benjamin?"

The winemaker mumbled a "yes," and then clearly said, "On one condition."

"What is that?" asked Elisabeth.

"I'm hungry. I'm starving, in fact. I'd like some paprika chicken with *galuskas*."

"With *what*?" Consuela jumped in.

Benjamin responded. "*Galuskas*: little pastas they make here, a sort of gnocchi, Miss Chavez."

"No need for such formality. You can call me Consuela."

"If you wish," the winemaker said. Actually, he didn't want to call her by her first name. She was such a flirt, he needed to keep her at arm's length.

The cab pulled up to the hotel, and Benjamin was relieved to end the conversation. He quickly got out and waited for the driver to remove the bags from the trunk. But before he could hand the driver a tip, the man pulled out a notepad and jotted something down.

"For you, pretty lady, if you need anything," the driver said, handing the paper to Consuela, who smiled and giggled, moving closer to Claude.

The menu at the Astoria restaurant offered paprika chicken, naturally, but without *galuskas*, the little dumplings Benjamin was pining for. He bit his tongue and didn't complain. Elisabeth and Consuela opted for *pörkölt*, a spicy stew that disappointed Elisabeth after a few mouthfuls. Consuela took just a couple forkfuls, as was her habit. Claude, as it happened, was just as famished as Benjamin and ordered duck breast stuffed with cheese. A cool riesling accompanied the feast.

Consuela didn't eat much, but she wasn't holding back on her drinking. After a few glasses she was hanging on Claude's shoulder and describing the sensuality of the *abrezo*, the embrace in tango dancing, and the *engache*, when a dancer wrapped her leg around her partner's. Consuela, it turned out, was a professional tango dancer.

"I have the blood *del pueblo argentino* flowing in my veins. I've danced the floors in Latin America, New York, and Montreal."

She went into a long discourse on the subtleties of the *cabeceo*, the technique of selecting dance partners from a distance, using eye contact and head movement.

"How did you meet?" Elisabeth asked, including Claude in the question.

"We met in Toulouse, the birthplace of the great Argentine singer Carlos Gardel," Consuela said.

"That's interesting. Your accent when you speak French almost sounds like you're from Toulouse or maybe from the Riviera," Elisabeth said.

Benjamin took note. His wife was sounding nonchalant, but she was suspicious.

"Claude, I've never known you to dance," Benjamin said.

"I don't. I was in town visiting an old friend, an author who had been drafted to judge a huge dance competition. It wasn't his thing, so he talked the organizing committee into giving me his place. He sold me as a bigwig in the publishing world, and they were all too happy to let me judge. My friend thought I might enjoy it."

"I guess you got to kiss the winner," Benjamin said.

"We were both staying at the Grand Hotel de l'Opéra on the Place du Capitole," Consuela said. "And soon we were in the same room!"

Benjamin glanced at Claude.

"Claude is so irresistible! And so cultured…"

Claude was quiet now. He listened as Consuela related their story: their night of lovemaking, their inability to be apart afterward, and the fact that Claude spoke Castilian.

Benjamin knew that Claude would never say anything about the previous love of his life. He was a gentleman, after all. But the winemaker was aware of one other important woman in Claude's life. Her name was Pilar, and Claude had met her in Seville, when he was a student backpacking across the Iberian Peninsula. It was there that he had learned to roll his tongue to the beat of the jota folkdance and how to kiss with the finesse of a matador. Pilar lived near the bullring in old Seville. She was a brunette and dark-skinned, and her eyes were the color of green water— like Consuela's.

By the time they finished their meal, there was no further talk of the cultural program that Claude had masterminded. In the magnificent Palace of Arts, with its Greek design, friezes, and caryatids, there was a painting exhibition, but neither Benjamin nor Elisabeth had any desire to run through the picture galleries with the other couple.

15

Elisabeth refused to let Benjamin call Bordeaux to check in and insisted that they start their sightseeing right away. Their first stop: Saint Stephen's Basilica, dedicated to the first king of Hungary. Once they were there, Benjamin found himself fascinated with its resemblance to Saint Paul's Cathedral in London. The winemaker held forth on the similarities—the central dome and two bell towers topped with pinnacles—until Elisabeth pulled him by the sleeve toward the back of the church to show him a strange relic. Set in a small glass box was the mummified hand of Saint Stephen.

"I read about this in one of the guidebooks, Benjamin. On Saint Stephen's Day every year, they take this hand out for a walk. Actually, it leads the annual parade. Do you believe it? When Stephen was canonized in the eleventh century, they exhumed his body and lopped off his arm. The hand wound up traveling all over Eastern Europe before winding up here. I don't know what happened to the rest of his arm. People who aren't so religious call it the monkey paw."

Benjamin examined the hand.

"Back then, people trafficked in relics," he said. "These days, they traffic in many other things."

He slipped a coin into the moneybox, and a light illuminated the mummified hand, which was curled in a fist.

The light went off after half a minute, and Benjamin turned to walk away. But before he could move, he spotted someone just to his right. It was a kid with unkempt raven-colored hair. He was holding out his hand. Startled, Benjamin didn't do anything. He looked like so many of the youths who hung out at tourist sites, yet his eyes had an unnerving intensity and he was smiling. Benjamin dug into his pocket for a coin and offered it to the boy. The kid took it, and Benjamin realized that he was actually much taller than a child. He looked like he was seventeen or eighteen years old. Maybe even twenty.

"Deutsch?" the supplicant asked.

Elisabeth shook her head.

"English?"

Benjamin's linen trousers and well-polished Lobb shoes had most likely given him away. Still, Benjamin told the youth that he was French.

"My English better than my *français*," the kid said.

He followed them out of the basilica, and in the sunlight there was no longer any question about the beggar's age. He was well past adolescence. Benjamin could see that he had an athletic build under his blue jogging suit. His pale yellow T-shirt sported the logo of a Budapest martial-arts club.

The young man was focused on Elisabeth.

"I know every place in Budapest. I'm a good guide. I was born here. Want to see bridges? I show you bridges. Want a *kavé*? I show you *kavé*."

He claimed to be a computer science student and a good soccer player. He dropped the name of the famous French player Zidane as a sort of golden ticket. But it would take more to convince Benjamin to see this rather roguish boy as an ally much less a friend.

Elisabeth, on the other hand, seemed quite susceptible to the charisma of the young man with an angelic face and a full head of lustrous black hair. She asked how much he would charge.

"No charge, ma'am," he said, flashing a smile. "I do it for pleasure."

Benjamin didn't believe that for a minute. He felt a tinge of annoyance when his wife took a twenty-euro note out of her purse and handed it over. Really? They were doing fine on their own.

"Thank you," the young man said, flashing yet another smile. "My name is Zoltán. I give you best tour ever."

His English was hardly flawless, but his mannerisms suggested a certain sensitivity and a semblance of education, too.

Benjamin wasn't quite comfortable with surrendering to Zoltán's guidance, but he grudgingly went along. He had promised Elisabeth a good vacation, and if this was what she wanted to do, so be it.

Zoltán led them out of the basilica, and as they descended the steps, Benjamin recognized a familiar face from the ship. It was the man with the sketchpad. He was standing in the square, and he appeared to be drawing the basilica.

"Honey, that man over there was on the ship with us," Benjamin said. "Let's go say hello."

He took Elisabeth's arm and walked over. The artist looked up, nodded, and stopped drawing.

"I see you're enjoying the sights," Benjamin said. "My name is Benjamin. This is my wife, Elisabeth, and…." Benjamin turned to introduce their guide, but Zoltán was nowhere to be seen.

"Oh, our tour guide seems to have disappeared," he said, turning to Elisabeth and giving her an I-told-you-so look.

"He's over there on the steps," Elisabeth whispered.

"I've been enjoying this sight in particular. Connor Adamson's the name," the man said, shaking Benjamin's hand and nodding to Elisabeth.

"May I have a look?" the winemaker asked. "I was admiring what you did on the ship. I used to be an artist myself."

Adamson handed him the sketchpad, and Benjamin and Elisabeth silently studied the man's drawings. "I can see you have a gift," he said after a few minutes.

"I don't know about that. It's just something I like to do when I'm traveling. I'm actually a graphic artist and do most of my work on the computer. So what brings you to Budapest?"

"We're visiting. Taking in the city before we move on to Tokaj. And you?"

"Just visiting, too. Being stuck behind the computer in England so much of the time, I like to get out and see the rest of Europe when I can."

"Are you staying at the Astoria?" Benjamin asked. "Perhaps we could meet for a drink later."

"Thanks, but I'm afraid I can't. I'm having dinner with my fiancée's cousin this evening."

"Is your fiancée traveling with you?"

"No, I'm afraid she's not." The smile vanished from the artist's face, and he looked back at his sketchpad. "She's in Syria."

"Oh," Benjamin said. "You must be very worried for her."

"Yes, but we're keeping in touch, and I'm trying to get her here safely. With some luck, she'll be with me soon."

"Well, then, I wish you the very best," Benjamin said. "We'll let you get back to your drawing."

Benjamin and Elisabeth said their good-byes and started heading in the other direction. Elisabeth looked around for Zoltán, who seemed to appear from nowhere.

"How awful for that poor man," Elisabeth said. "And his fiancée! He must be terribly distressed."

"I imagine so," Benjamin answered. "The conflict in Syria and the refugee situation are heart-wrenching. I'm sure he wants to get her to Europe as quickly and easily as possible." He turned to Zoltán. "Zoltán, you should have stayed with us. That artist is quite skilled. He's penned a perfect sketch of you. So, you promised us a tour. Shall we get on with it?"

Zoltán shot a glance at the artist. Turning back to his clients, he raised his arms and ushered them in the other direction. "This way."

He led his clients from one memorable spot the next. Elisabeth especially enjoyed the Central Market Hall, where she admired the embroidered textiles and purchased some paprika. After several hours of sightseeing, however, she was worn out, and Benjamin needed to catch his breath. Only their tour guide appeared to be indefatigable. Elisabeth suggested cooling off with a soft drink, and Benjamin pointed to the terrace of a large café. Zoltán dissuaded him.

"*Kavé* for tourists! Borozo better."

Elisabeth consulted her smartphone. "It's a bar, dear. I'm all right with that. Are you?"

Benjamin nodded, and the Cookers let themselves be steered to the end of a narrow street. They entered a tavern that wasn't much to look at. The walls were painted blue, and the few sticky tables were being used as armrests by the old folk who were riveted to a plasma-screen TV, where an important soccer game was playing out.

Elisabeth ordered a soft drink. Benjamin was about to order for himself, but Zoltán placed a hand on his wrist, as if to say the winemaker should trust him. They were friends, after all, weren't they?

A beautiful blonde with Slavic eyes took a ladle and filled two glasses with a yellowish liquid that hardly looked drinkable.

The two men clinked their glasses and raised them to their lips. Zoltán grinned. Benjamin sipped, winced, and turned to his wife.

"It's a dry furmint, a white Hungarian grape variety that's only made here. Elisabeth, my dear, why don't you put a bottle in our luggage. It'll come in handy for unclogging the sinks at Grangebelle."

16

When the Cooker couple, saddled with their guide, met up with Claude and Consuela in the salon of the Hotel Astoria, Benjamin realized that his friend's mistress had gotten her way yet again. Better to wander and "capture the soul of a city," she had said, than to waste the day in poorly ventilated museums. Benjamin couldn't help noticing that she had several shopping bags.

Indeed, Consuela had spent much of her time in high-end boutiques and had picked up some Herend porcelain—charged on Claude's credit card, most certainly.

"You know boutique-hopping isn't my thing," Claude told Benjamin. "So I went off by myself to experience some of Budapest's quaint cafés."

"What did you find?"

"I went to the Gerbeaud first."

"How was it?"

"Too much like the Café de Flore and Les Deux Magots in Paris—spoiled by writers and intellectuals who used to gather there to brag and promote their latest pack of lies. They're tourist haunts now. I managed to stay half an hour. Then enough was enough."

A Hungarian friend who worked in film had told him to check out the café Spinoza and the Eckermann, but he had only walked by them, not bothering to stop and taste the mousse or the famous coffee. These meccas of the Budapest intelligentsia had modernized, which bothered Claude enormously. The Internet had woven its web everywhere. Computer screens had replaced the chessboards and decks of cards. Claude missed the days when cafés smelled of absinthe and patrons pondered their moves in a cloud of smoke.

"I finally found salvation at the New York Café, a space so ornate, it almost seems magical. I wish you had been with me, Benjamin. You would have loved it—the crystal chandeliers and the ceiling adorned with Gustav Mannheimer and Franz Eisenhut paintings. The brass banisters are covered with red velvet that match the upholstery on the chairs. I've never seen a café as elegant."

While Claude was detailing his explorations, Consuela was busy showing off her purchases. Benjamin glanced at Elisabeth and could see boredom written all over her face. His wife enjoyed shopping as much as anyone else, but it didn't consume her.

Zoltán was taking it all in with an almost silly smile. Elisabeth, realizing that she hadn't introduced their tour guide, interrupted the separate narratives.

Claude had an amused expression on his face as he appraised the man, whose jogging suit clashed with the posh ambiance of the Astoria. Consuela, meanwhile, was sizing him up the way a woman of experience might scrutinize her prey. Then, turning to Claude, she said in her native tongue, "*¡Cuerpo de los dioses con ojos asesinos!*"

Benjamin's rudimentary Spanish allowed him to sense the brute sexuality that Consuela saw in this boy. He was sensual and dangerous at the same time. Benjamin was a bit wary, and he noticed that Claude was giving their guide a suspicious look.

Yet Zoltán had impressed Benjamin with historical and architectural information that an ordinary person wouldn't have known if he hadn't studied somewhere. He had a rustic simplicity that appealed to the winemaker and even more so to his wife. His smile was warm, and his teeth were straight, and although Benjamin was no style expert, he was aware that Zoltán's goatee was on trend.

Benjamin was becoming convinced that Zoltán was not a city boy. His mannerisms betrayed him. He was almost certainly one of those kids from the countryside who came to Budapest—or Prague, Bucharest, or Warsaw—to seek a better life. Ironically, it was hardly an admirable life.

They were ready to deal drugs, fleece tourists, and beg and prostitute themselves.

The day had been exhausting. The Cookers wanted to dine alone in a restaurant in town. Claude and Consuela planned to do the same. That left Zoltán, and it was time to say good-bye.

"I'll come back tomorrow. Take you to Gellért baths."

Benjamin hesitated but finally agreed to the guide's proposition. They would meet at ten the next morning. He was about to send Zoltán off, but Consuela didn't seem ready to see him go. In fact, she hadn't taken her eyes off him.

"Claude, why don't we have a glass of Champagne with the tour guide? He might tell us something we don't know about Budapest."

Claude exchanged a glance with Benjamin, and the winemaker read the resignation in his eyes. Faced with this *fait accompli*, Claude acquiesced.

"Benjamin, before you head up to your room, could you spare me a cigar?" Claude asked. "I'm running out of fuel."

"Romeo y Julieta, Exhibición No. 4. Willthat do?"

Claude looked from his mistress to the young man, who was staring back at her.

"How could any cigar be more fitting?" he answered, taking it.

At eight o'clock, when the elegantly dressed Cookers came down to the hotel lobby to catch a cab to the Múzeum, the restaurant they had their hearts set on, Consuela, Zoltán, and Claude were still at the bar. All three were laughing. The Champagne was apparently breaking down the language barriers and sweeping away Claude's misgivings, if only temporarily. Benjamin recognized the golden neck of a vintage Dom Pérignon in the ice bucket. At least Consuela was faithful to something.

Dinner at the Múzeum was sumptuous and lavish. Benjamin ordered duck breast with green peppercorns and walnut-bread soufflé. Elisabeth had a delicious meal of veal *paprikasch* that she praised so highly, the chef told her his secret.

"You need lard and to add the sweet paprika before anything else."

"Yes," Elisabeth said. "That will bring out its flavor."

"I see you're an accomplished cook, Madam."

When she told him they were from Bordeaux, the chef's face lit up.

"Yes, Bordeaux! Château Margaux!"

That was just about all he knew about Michel de Montaigne's birthplace. Still, the chef, his oiled mustache, and his Magyar accent, had added charm to this dinner copiously washed down with wine from the Matra Mountains.

After dessert, Benjamin took several minutes to admire the Károly Lotz frescos on the high ceilings of the nineteenth-century restaurant. The trip was beginning to feel like the proverbial *Hungarian*

Rhapsody. Elisabeth was enjoying herself, and Benjamin was finally relaxing. Leaving the restaurant he put his arm around his wife's shoulder and kissed her neck. The night air was sweet.

The hotel lobby at that hour was practically deserted. Alone at the bar, Consuela and Zoltán were clearly drunk. They were laughing noisily and exchanging lustful looks. Benjamin figured Claude was back in his room, too inebriated to fret about his girlfriend's antics.

17

"You sure picked a good time to go dancing on the Volga, boss."

"The Volga is in Russia, Virgile."

"That doesn't change the fact that the shit has hit the fan here, and I'm having a hard time cleaning it up!"

"Calm down, son. Tell me what's going on."

"There's a bit of a bottleneck in the lab."

"Our lab is always filled with bottlenecks, isn't it?"

"This is no time for jokes. I'm the one who's back here trying to manage our clients. And they're not too happy right now."

To respond to his assistant's cry for help, Benjamin had chosen to sit in a wood-trimmed armchair in the far corner of the marble-filled lobby. Virgile's panicky voice kept Benjamin from admiring the large vase in the nearby wall niche. His shoulder muscles were tensing up.

Virgile continued. "Ladevèze is doing what he can, but he's not as familiar with the procedures as Alexandrine. And he's slower. Our clients are waiting too long for the results of their analyses. They're quite vexed with us at Saint Émilion and Pomerol!"

"Use Didier then."

"Yeah, right! Didier's already kissing up to our vintners with mildew. I'm not going to let him near our other clients too."

"You're being a bit harsh, aren't you?"

"He's not what you think, sir. He's always sweet-talking someone, always trying to cut corners and cheat people. And he's got a temper."

"You sound jealous. It's not very becoming."

"Boss, did you know that he was hanging around the lab last month? He was asking Alexandrine all kinds of questions. At first I thought he was hitting on her, but he was being so…"

"So what?"

"Disrespectful. I heard him say he'd never consider…"

"Consider what?"

"Well, okay, you asked. He didn't understand how she could be gay. Actually, he used the word dyke. He told her he'd never consider screwing a guy."

"You're right, that's not very professional, is it? Her personal life is none of his business."

"Oh, Alex handled it perfectly, as usual. She just told him he hadn't met the right man yet."

Benjamin chuckled. "Okay, Virgile, he's a bit rough around the edges, but he's good at what he does."

"That's not the end of the story, boss. Afterward, I saw them arguing. In any case, I don't trust him. As long as I'm here and you're there, I'm going to keep him reined in. Is that clear?"

Benjamin raised his eyebrows at Virgile's tone, but he didn't say anything. He studied an enormous bouquet of fresh flowers, all white, leaving Virgile time to calm down.

"Boss? You still there?"

"What about Alexandrine?"

"What about Alexandrine? I already told you she'll be out of work for a while. Her attacker really did a number on her."

"Will any of her injuries be permanent?"

"According to the doctors, her sensory organs weren't affected. The optic nerve is fine, but she'll need some rehabilitation."

"And her nose?"

"Broken. Don't worry. Plastic surgery does wonders these days. As far as her eyebrow ridge is concerned, the guy didn't go easy: three fractures!"

"Poor thing," Benjamin said.

"She is a bit depressed, but she should be able to leave the hospital soon."

"She'll still need our help, Virgile."

"I'm doing what I can, boss. But I'm stretched thin, and, as I said, I don't trust Didier with our clients. There's so much to do at Cooker & Co., and the work is piling up."

"I understand, son. As soon as I get back your workload will ease up. By the way, has her companion been staying with her at the hospital?"

"Let's talk about that so-called friend. She hasn't been seen or heard from. Alexandrine finally came clean. Her girlfriend left her a week ago without so much as a by-your-leave. Excellent timing, right?"

"Hmm, interesting," Benjamin murmured.

"Boss, are you thinking what I'm thinking? I wouldn't be surprised if it was her girlfriend who attacked her."

"You're jumping to conclusions, Virgile."

"Have you ever seen chicks fight? When they go at it, it's worse than guys."

"I don't know, Virgile. Alexandrine had such a good Bordeaux upbringing. It's hard to imagine her in a scuffle of any kind."

"Well, in any case, I asked her out front, but she… Well, to be honest, she didn't really answer. I get the feeling there's a lot about Alexandrine that we don't know."

"Just see what you can find out. Keep going to the hospital. Keep talking to her. She trusts you. You might turn up a lead." Benjamin decided to change the subject. "All right, what about the mildew situation? What's going on with that? Other than your suspicions about Didier, that is."

"It's spreading, boss. It's been stormy here. The rains have hit Bergerac, Duras, the Haut Médoc,

Blaye, and Entre-deux-Mers. Graves isn't quite as wet, but that's not saying much. It's gotten to the fruit in quite a few vineyards. I haven't seen anything like this in a long time."

"Unfortunately, some winegrowers refuse to use copper sulfate," Benjamin said.

"Well, the number of ecologically minded winemakers has risen. Besides, spraying is expensive, and winegrowers save money when they cut down. But, when there's extensive damage, some go running back to the old methods."

Like a physician sure of his diagnosis, the Bordeaux wine expert dictated his fungicidal treatment. He detailed each agent and exactly how much to use.

"That's what I've been doing, boss."

"If you want my opinion, son, I don't think the storms will be the last of our bad weather. The forecasters are predicting another heat wave."

18

The next day, the Cookers ran into Claude in the hallway on their way down to the lobby.

"Consuela's running behind schedule. Why don't we have a cup of coffee while we wait?"

"Did she have a late night?" Benjamin asked. "We saw her at the bar when we came in around eleven. I take it you turned in early."

"Yes. The conversation wasn't all that scintillating. When I left, she was telling that guide about everyone from the cruise, in minute detail. To tell the truth, I expected her in much later, but she stumbled back to the room around midnight. I felt a bit sorry for the kid. Ship gossip wouldn't be the kind of thing a kid like him would be interested in, I'd think."

Elisabeth gave Benjamin a look. It wasn't the conversation that intrigued Zoltán.

"I could use some breakfast. I'm starving," Elisabeth said.

Claude led Benjamin and Elisabeth into the restaurant, with its crystal chandeliers and mirrored walls, and a hostess seated them next to the American couple who had been on the same boat from Vienna. They smiled politely and focused on the menu. Just as they were about to order coffee and pastries, the man leaned over.

"Did you hear?" he asked.

"Hear what?" Benjamin said.

"The police were in earlier. They were showing a picture around. It was the artist from the boat. The guy with the beard."

"Why?"

"They found his body near Saint Stephen's Basilica. Shot dead. It happened last night. Sometime between ten and two in the morning."

Benjamin glanced at his wife and grabbed her hand.

"We saw him drawing outside the basilica yesterday. We even went over and talked with him. He said his name was Connor Adamson. He was visiting his fiancée's cousin here."

"I can't believe it," Elisabeth said, looking stunned.

Benjamin sighed. "His fiancée will be devastated. Do the police have a motive? A robbery gone bad?"

"I don't know," the American said.

At that moment, Consuela, pale, bleary-eyed, and looking annoyed, made her way to the table. She gulped a cup of café au lait and said she was ready to leave.

They found Zoltán waiting for them in the lobby. He looked chipper in a brand-name black jogging suit. He was also wearing an expensive-looking pair of athletic shoes.

Zoltán grinned and suggested that they take the tram instead of taxis.

"It's funnier," he said.

This made the winemaker smile. He didn't want to object, as Elisabeth still seemed shaken.

"I feel better with somebody who knows the city, Benjamin," Elisabeth whispered, taking her husband's arm. "He reminds me a bit of Virgile. Do you get the same impression?"

"Now that you mention it," Benjamin answered. "He's certainly a bright young man."

The tram was packed, and a number of passengers were forced to stand. In an unusually tender gesture, Consuela put her head on Claude's shoulder. Benjamin glanced at Zoltán, who was looking the other way, as if he and Consuela hadn't spent the previous evening flirting with each other.

In less than ten minutes the four tourists were standing before the art nouveau façade of the Hotel Gellért. Benjamin and Claude took in every architectural detail. Elisabeth and Consuela went straight into the lobby, which was filled with mosaics and sculpted columns.

They purchased the tickets to the thermal baths. The men and women went to their separate changing areas: large blue-tiled vestibules lined with cubicles that didn't lock. A prevailing atmosphere of body heat diminished any sense of modesty. Armed with their terrycloth towels, Benjamin, Claude, and their chatty guide joined Elisabeth and Consuela in the large pool. The water was hot and almost turquoise. No one was actually swimming. Instead, the bathers were luxuriating in an atmosphere of muted elegance.

Elisabeth pointed to the glass ceiling. "So much light's coming through. It's superb. Zoltán, didn't you tell us that baths like these are actually part of the health-care system and that doctors think the spring water's medicinal?"

Zoltán nodded. "Budapest has almost two dozen thermal baths. The Gellért's is the grandest. People come here not only to spend time in the water—it's always thirty-eight degrees Celsius—but also to get massages and go in the sauna. Look," he said, gesturing toward a board game, "you can even play chess while you're here."

Benjamin asked Claude if he'd like to start a game.

Elisabeth and Consuela talked quietly. Zoltán was showing off his muscled torso as he floated in the water. He smiled at the women from time to time without getting too close.

After an hour in the pool, Elisabeth and Consuela got out to have some mint tea. Benjamin, who had lost his match against Claude, was keeping an eye on Zoltán. The tour guide seemed to be in familiar territory. Zoltán, too, had emerged from the water and had walked over to a group of older men, who seemed quite interested in him. So, was the boy selling his body regularly in order to buy his expensive shoes and pay for his gym membership?

Benjamin had read about the infamous Ergo insurance sex party in the Gellért baths. The boy would be foolish to drum up any business here, considering all the surveillance the hotel probably had by now. But maybe he was risking it and giving these men his contact information. Zoltán's guided tours evidently had back-room options.

When Benjamin told his wife what he was thinking, Elisabeth glanced at Zoltán and agreed. Consuela, however, didn't believe it.

"He's one hundred percent hetero, I'm telling you. I know them well, the ones who swim both ways."

Elisabeth corrected her with a giggle. "You mean swing."

"Swing, if you prefer, although here swim is more appropriate," Consuela said, throwing her damp black mane over a shoulder.

"Shush," Elisabeth said. "He's coming our way."

Sure enough, Zoltán was approaching them, his stretchable polyester bathing suit hardly concealing his virility.

After telling him that they'd be happy to stay a little longer, Elisabeth invited Zoltán to join them for tea. He accepted.

Benjamin was always impressed with his wife's ability to get information from people. She made it seem effortless. Benjamin listened as Elisabeth questioned Zoltán about his past and present. As he suspected, Zoltán was not a city boy. He had been in Budapest for a year and lived with his elderly and half-crazy aunt. He was from Szerencs, a godforsaken town in eastern Hungary.

"Tokaj, you know?" he asked Elisabeth.

No, his parents were not winemakers. His mother did housecleaning, while his disabled father could only contribute his income from a pension and the meager amount he made on the garden vegetables he sold at market. But his Uncle Antal and cousins Pavel and Vilmos all worked in the vineyards and made a very good wine.

"Gold wine!" he insisted, as if he were ready to divulge some magic formula for a price.

As Zoltán continued his story, Benjamin glanced at Consuela. She was staring at the boy while discreetly rimming her cup with the tip of her tongue. Zoltán didn't seem to notice. How pathetic, Benjamin thought.

From the corner of his eye, Benjamin noticed another young man. He had just winked at Zoltán. The tour guide's face tensed, and he suggested that they get dressed. They had more to see.

The couples reunited in the hotel lobby a half hour later. Exiting the building, they hailed two cabs. Destination: Margaret Island. Zoltán climbed in with the Cookers and commented on all the buildings they passed. At the Margaret Bridge, he explained that this scrap of metal spanning the Danube was the work of a French engineer.

"Eiffel?" Benjamin asked.

"No, he only built towers," Zoltán answered. Benjamin didn't bother to correct him.

The cab came to a stop, and Benjamin and Elisabeth got out. But before the winemaker could pull out his money to pay, a frantic Claude came running up. A giant in dark glasses and leather was by his side, demanding immediate payment for the cab ride.

When Claude had reached into his pocket, he discovered that his wallet, credit cards, and passport were missing. Benjamin tried to appease the cab driver, but he couldn't make himself heard above Consuela's shrieking. She was livid—not that her lover had been robbed, but that he was inconveniencing her.

Benjamin paid both drivers and appealed to everyone to remain calm. Zoltán looked indignant and said he knew the address of the French Embassy.

"No panic," the boy kept telling Consuela, but she wasn't hearing it. She looked ready to slap him. Benjamin shook his head. When would his friend come to his senses and dump this woman?

19

"So, boss, how's it going?"

"Not exactly *la dolce vita*, I fear."

The winemaker told Virgile that Claude's problems had sapped much of the joy from their trip. First, he had chosen to come with a vixen. Then he had been robbed. Claude had filed a complaint with the police and had contacted a higher-up at the French embassy, thanks to Benjamin's connections.

"His lady friend is furious that he had to cancel his credit cards. That limits her spending—at least until he gets replacements. And to think, we have yet to taste a drop of Tokaji."

"How's Mrs. Cooker?"

"She sends you her best and keeps telling me that I'm unbelievably fortunate to have such an intelligent and efficient assistant. I'm inclined to agree with her. You might even see that reflected in your next paycheck. So, what about Alexandrine?"

"She'll be out of the hospital tomorrow. But I don't think she'll be able to go home."

"What?"

"She told me she was afraid. Her voice was shaking, and she was almost crying. She thought the person would be waiting for her."

"I don't understand. If it was a random mugger at the parking garage near the office, she has nothing to fear at home."

"Exactly. Yesterday I was chatting with a nurse at the hospital—"

"Spare me the details of your conquests, Virgile."

"It wasn't like that, boss. We were just having a coffee during her break. I was waiting for Alexandrine to wake up from a nap. Anyway, the nurse works at the hospital's center for victims of violence. I rather led her to believe that Alexandrine was family, and she suggested that her behavior seemed more like that of long-term abuse than a simple mugging."

"So you mean her girlfriend could be abusive?"

"I don't know, but the story hasn't added up from the beginning. I'm pretty sure she was attacked at her home."

"So what is she going to do?"

"Well, um, I invited her to stay at my place for a night."

"Virgile!"

"What, boss?"

"Well, please reassure me that you have no girlfriends there now."

"Of course I don't. Boss, she feels safe with me. It's the least I can do."

"No funny business, do you hear me?"

"Boss! First you want me to take care of her, then you don't. Have a little faith in me."

"Your reputation does precede you. Keep me posted, in any case. Tomorrow we'll be leaving the Danube and traveling by train."

20

The Budapest Keleti train station was a door to the Orient. Under its canopy, the Orient Express and the Bartók Béla set out to conquer the large plains of the Great East. Claude had told Benjamin that taking the train to the Tokaj region would be more enjoyable than renting a car. Once they arrived, they would see where they stood.

Though not quite smiling, Claude didn't seem unhappy to be leaving Budapest. Consuela, who had been furious with her lover the previous day, was lavishing him with affection. Elisabeth, meanwhile, couldn't hide her delight in taking the train, which, in a single night, could reduce Europe to a mere jigsaw puzzle.

Elisabeth had always preferred taking the train to flying. She still had fond memories of the Transcantábrico in Spain, the Blaue Wagen in Germany, the Golden Mountain and the Rheingold in Switzerland, the BB Blue in Austria, and, of course, the princely Royal Scotsman in Great Britain, which was Benjamin's favorite.

Actually, even in luxury trains, comfort was rarely at the level one read about in novels, but the staff was always assiduous, the cutlery spotless, the napkins well ironed, and the wine list extensive.

It was an opportunity to watch the scenery parade by: deep valleys, armies of holm oak trees, steep and eternally snow-covered peaks, endless green pastures, churches with bell towers, and houses perched on the riverbanks. Elisabeth loved all of it, and Benjamin did too.

Zoltán was with them, even though Benjamin and Claude had their doubts. The theft of Claude's things had shaken their confidence. But Consuela had suggested it, and Elisabeth had remained a loyal supporter of their tour guide.

"That young man was sent to us from heaven!" she had argued. "Claude could have been robbed anywhere in Europe. It didn't have anything to do with Zoltán. Let's stop being suspicious. We could use his help."

The five of them were in the same compartment. Consuela and Elisabeth were taking in the scenery. Claude was reading his manuscript again, although he still wasn't engrossed. Benjamin was directly across from Zoltán, silently staring at him. Zoltán was sitting straight and holding the winemaker's gaze. The winemaker had paid the guide's train ticket, and, in exchange, Zoltán had spontaneously tended to the baggage and gotten cold drinks for his clients. Consuela may have suggested the guide come along, but she had objected to giving him her bags.

"*¡Gato escaldado del agua fria rehuye,*" Consuela had whispered.

"We're hardly scalded cats getting dunked in cold water," Elisabeth had responded in a tone that surprised her husband.

"I believe the translation for that is 'once bitten, twice shy,'" Claude said, taking his own bag.

Hungary was now unveiling its monotonous agrarian landscape. The train rolled past patches of corn, geometric orchards, sparsely populated villages, teams of animals, and scattered pieces of farm equipment.

At certain moments, Claude seemed worried. He'd clutch the manuscript he was marking up with a red felt pen and look out the window.

"I'm surprised you still work on paper," Benjamin said, trying to get his friend's mind off his concerns. "Don't you all work on computers these days?"

"Yes, we do," Claude answered. "But old habits die hard, and every once in a while I like to do it this way. You should appreciate that, Benjamin. You prefer paper too."

The air conditioning wasn't working properly, and Benjamin loosened his collar. He had to admit it—the train, named for the famous Hungarian composer, wasn't as luxurious as he had hoped.

A few minutes later, the Bartók Béla slowed, and the conductor announced the Szerencs station.

When it came to a stop, several people boarded, including two old women in scarves who were carrying shopping bags overflowing with vegetables. They peeked into the compartment to see if there was room. Zoltán intervened, telling them firmly that it was full. The old ladies muttered and walked off.

The train resumed its easterly course, and soon the landscape changed. The boring fields gave way to a valley planted with wide rows of vines. Tokaj could not be far away.

The train marched by a handful of villages clumped around churches. Benjamin thought he recognized the Disznókó estate and beyond it, the grands crus Deák, Szarvas, and Hétszóló leading to the verdant skirts of Tokaj, with its magical volcanic soil.

The winemaker glanced at Zoltán. He seemed to be regarding this familiar horizon with a feeling of belonging but also reserve. The guide pointed out the other villages, the roads leading to the whitewashed wine warehouses, and the various properties. Benjamin was already familiar with the region's rivers: the Bodrog and the Tisza, which, like the Ciron tributary of the Garonne in Sauternes country, created a perfect environment for the *botrytis cinerea* fungus responsible for the noble rot on grapes when the conditions were right, resulting in some of the world's finest dessert wines.

When they came out of the small train station, Zoltán fiercely negotiated the taxi fare to the inn and from there to the top of Mount Tokaj. Scowling, the driver crammed the luggage into the back of the station wagon. Fortunately, the inn was on the way to Bodrogkeresztúr, only two or three kilometers from the train station.

The inn was actually a yellow house with seven bedrooms. There was no real décor, just the embroidered curtains on the tiny windows. But the place exuded cleanliness and hospitality. Benjamin thought the accommodations would be perfectly fine.

Consuela wanted to rest in her room. Claude was tempted to stay with her, but exploring the countryside was an itch he needed to scratch. The Cookers, meanwhile, were eager to get to the vineyards. Didn't their guide want to introduce them to his cousins Pavel and Vilmos?

The taxi driver was waiting outside the inn. He and Zoltán were joking now, looking thick as thieves. Benjamin regretted not seeing right through the boy's act at the train station. Zoltán and the driver were bent on taking them for a ride. But the winemaker wasn't having it. He was nobody's fool, and this driver, Gábor, wouldn't get one more forint out of him.

When they reached their destination, Benjamin and Claude contemplated the panorama from the slope of Mount Tokaj. Zoltán stayed at Elisabeth's side, pointing out the Zemplén Mountains, which were covered with oak trees used to make the barrels. Looming in the distance were the Carpathian Mountains.

"Dracula Castle," Zoltán said. He grinned, and with alarming familiarity, he leaned in and feigned a desire to bite Elisabeth's neck. Benjamin, who had turned around to join her, almost rushed over to intervene.

"Our guide has quite a sense of humor," Elisabeth said when he reached her.

Zoltán continued his commentary with charm and spontaneity. He indicated the contours of the Bodrogzug wildlife protection area and pointed to some large birds circling in the air.

"Black storks here," he said.

"No, really?" Elisabeth was incredulous. "I've never seen black storks before. Have you, Benjamin?"

The winemaker shrugged.

Their guide continued his narrative as if he were the master of this playground of his childhood. He told them about the Bodrog, the unfaithful river that would abandon its course in the springtime and flood the fields. The lowlands would become big muddy lakes covering everything. The region's seasonal wetness and the foggy weather that followed were actually the winegrowers' secret weapons. Combined, they created prime conditions for noble rot. The infected grapes, if picked at just the right moment, produced an especially fine and concentrated sweet wine.

Benjamin almost wished he had made the trip during Indian summer, when winegrowers would dare to predict the harvest. What they needed at that point was a wind from the great plains of Russia to raisinate the grapes—to dry them up like raisins, concentrating the sugar content.

Here, in northeastern Hungary, the interplay of moisture and sunshine stoked by the winds of the Ural Mountains produced the only grape of its kind in the world, as well as the most expensive. Its name was aszú, meaning desiccated.

Benjamin had taken over the commentary. He was on familiar turf now, where Zoltán could not rival him.

"On the face of this earth I don't know of any wine that has more residual sugar than the Tokaji produced here," Benjamin said. The great Yquem vintages have 100 to 150 grams per liter, while the sweetest Tokaji—the eszencia—has more than 450 grams per liter. Some exceptional vintages can have as much as 900 grams per liter."

"That's enough to make my teeth hurt," Claude responded.

"That's why it's called dessert wine," Benjamin said. "When the grapes reach maturity, they have a rather low sugar concentration but high acidity. It's not until the end of September, when the grapes reach true overripeness and botrytis, and

95

the raisinating occurs, that the high sugar content is reached. The result is liquid gold."

"I told you, gold wine," Zoltán enthused.

By now the afternoon heat had cleared the haze shrouding the countryside. Both Elisabeth and Claude had taken off the wide-brimmed hats they had brought with them. Zoltán had shed the zippered top of his jogging suit. Benjamin, the traditionalist, however, was still in his corduroy jacket. It wasn't the heat that was bothering him. It was his hunger. He wanted to return to the hotel and get something to eat.

But before the winemaker could usher his companions back to the cab, his cell phone vibrated. He didn't recognize the number.

"Mr. Cooker?"

"Speaking."

"This is the office of the French ambassador to Hungary."

The winemaker recognized the voice of the man who had been so affable the previous day, when he had helped Claude handle his difficulties.

"Please hold for the ambassador."

In less than a minute he heard another voice.

"Mr. Cooker, I'm delighted to speak with you. I love the *Cooker Guide*. It's my Bible. How is your visit going? Better than yesterday, I hope."

"I'm on Mount Tokaj."

"Hungary's Mount Athos, except the monasteries here are underground in a vast system of cellars carved out of solid rock between 1400 and 1600, and the holy wine, I believe, is the most expensive in the world—and the oldest botrytized wine there is."

"To be honest, Mr. Ambassador, I've yet to take communion today."

The French ambassador laughed and then fell silent. "There's some news concerning your friend, or at least concerning his passport."

"Yes? Please go on."

"Mr. Nithard's passport was recovered by Hungarian police during an unrelated arrest in Budapest yesterday. It was in the possession of a Syrian national. We don't know exactly what he intended to do with it, but we suspect that he planned to doctor the document."

"For what purposes, Mr. Ambassador?"

"We think he was going to sell it on the black market. Considering everything that's going on now, a French passport can fetch a lot of money. The police are questioning the man, and we might have more information later. Meanwhile, Mr. Nithard should be able to continue traveling safely on the emergency passport we issued yesterday. I wish you all the best, Mr. Cooker. And if you come through Budapest on your way home, I'd be delighted to have a glass of wine with our country's leading wine authority."

"It would be a pleasure, sir." Benjamin ended the call.

"Why are you staring at me?" Claude asked.

"Claude, you promised me a delightful cruise along the Danube and a leisurely stroll through the vines. But you never told me there'd be so much intrigue."

Claude broke into a grin. "Benjamin, you're a fine one to talk about intrigue."

21

Virgile knew that Alexandrine had a lovely apartment next to the Quinconces Esplanade, and from her balcony one could almost touch the winged woman atop the Girondins Monument. Although he had never been there, he could envision the high ceilings, the sweeping drapes, the Louis XVI chests of drawers, the large mantelpieces above the fireplaces, the chandeliers, the old-fashioned parquet floors, the Oriental rugs, and the walls covered with faded wallpaper that needed to be replaced.

Virgile also knew that Alexandrine's finances wouldn't allow for any restoration. Most of her salary was going toward upkeep.

He had just walked past the colossal statues of philosophers Michel de Montaigne and Montesquieu and had positioned himself to see the entrance to Alexandrine's apartment building. He knew exactly where it was, having attended more than one event on the massive square lined with trees and picturesque streetlamps, which at nighttime gave the promenade a magical aura. Alexandrine had pointed out her windows at the last wine festival they attended together.

Because Alexandrine was afraid to go home, Virgile wanted to assess the danger for himself. He settled himself in under the trees and took out his tablet to catch up on reports. He looked up from time to time, watching the door.

He spent the whole morning there and didn't notice anything out of the ordinary. There were the usual passersby, parents with young children, a few teenagers trying to look cool, and an older man camped out on a park bench. He looked too well dressed to be a bum, but too unkempt to be sober.

Just as his stomach was beginning to grumble and he was about to go get some lunch, Virgile did a double take. A man he recognized was trying to get in the building.

22

Gábor got his forints. He did his best to win an extra tip, but Benjamin stood his ground. Zoltán indicated with a gesture that haggling would get the driver nowhere. The taxi disappeared in a cloud of dust.

"I'm thirsty and very hungry," Claude said.

"I'm famished too, my friend. Let's see what we can find to eat."

When Consuela came down to meet them, Claude told her about the phone call from the ambassador.

"A Syrian national had your passport?" she asked.

"I imagine with everyone leaving Syria, an altered French passport could go for thousands of euros," Claude said.

"As much as ten thousand," Consuela corrected.

Benjamin, Claude, and Elisabeth all turned and looked at her.

"I read it in the paper," Consuela added, giving them a coy smile.

"Let's not think about that now," Benjamin said. "We're on vacation. Right?" They took a table under an arbor. The bees were too occupied with gathering pollen to notice the diners, who were basking in the warmth and admiring the view. Below, the Tokaji vines were unfurling like green ribbons.

Benjamin ordered a Zempléni sauvignon blanc. The dry white, served at eight degrees centigrade, had a smoky aroma that delighted the men. The women weren't quite as impressed. After a few sips, however, Elisabeth began to appreciate the subtle notes of citrus and green apple and the well-controlled acidity.

"It's surprisingly fresh," Elisabeth finally said.

The meal included copious servings of freshwater fish soup. Consuela had dropped her diva airs and seemed genuine for a change, while the wine had loosened Claude's tongue. Benjamin was feeling better with each bite, but he said nothing.

"Benjamin, you're being very quiet," Elisabeth said, interrupting her husband's musings.

"Just enjoying myself, dear," he answered, patting Elisabeth's hand.

Despite Elisabeth's urgings, Zoltán hadn't joined them for lunch. Instead, he left to eat with his cousins Pavel and Vilmos. Then he wanted to see a young lady from Szerencs about a business matter. Elisabeth took this to mean an old love affair. Their tour guide promised to return later to take them to the wine cellars.

The Cookers and Claude and Consuela were fine with that. They were in no hurry. Tokaj was at their feet, and that was all that mattered.

"One week might not be long enough," Benjamin said as he enjoyed an aszú sorbet, made from the world-famous, topaz-colored sweet wine. "Unfortunately, there's too much going on in Bordeaux for me to extend our stay. I'll need to get back before things really get out of hand."

23

After grabbing a *jambon-beurre* sandwich from a bakery, Virgile went back to his apartment and surveyed the chaos. There was no way he could invite a woman into his place, much less Alexandrine de La Palussière. His was a true bachelor's haunt, and his liaisons almost always took place elsewhere.

Now, however, he had to do something. He sighed and got to it, racing through the rooms, dumping the dirty laundry into the hamper, throwing away the trash, doing the dishes, and cleaning out the refrigerator.

An hour later, his pad was still badly in need of a sense of style, but it was clean enough. Alexandrine could set foot in it. He took a final look before locking the door behind him and heading off to Saint André Hospital, where he found Alexandrine waiting for him, her things neatly packed in a bag.

She declined a wheelchair and took Virgile's arm, drawing closer when they got outside. On first glance, anyone would have thought they looked like lovers. But then the passerby would have noted that Alexandrine was clutching her companion like a lost child, and she was hiding her face behind her hair and dark sunglasses. Nothing, however, could conceal the unsightly bandage on her nose.

"Is everyone staring, Virgile?" Alexandrine asked, nervously checking out each person they encountered.

"No one is staring, Alexandrine. Everyone else is too self-absorbed to give you a second look."

They walked in silence until they reached Virgile's car, which was parked under a fragrant linden tree. Alexandrine's face relaxed, and she smiled.

"Even under this bandage I can smell it, Virgile."

The moment passed. Alexandrine got in the car and made sure the door was locked. Large drops of rain were slapping the windshield, but Virgile didn't turn on the wipers.

"The rain will pass. It's headed east."

When Virgile unlocked the door to his apartment, Alexandrine took off her sunglasses. Her eyes were glistening with tears, and Virgile could see the relief on her face. He led her to a chair and helped her sit down.

"Somebody left something for you," she said, pointing to the door.

Virgile looked back and saw an envelope with a heart drawn on it. Someone had slipped it under the door. He walked over and picked it up. Without giving the envelope any attention, he slipped it into the pocket of his jeans.

"So, you have a stalker?" Alexandrine said, smiling.

"One of many," Virgile answered, grinning back at Alexandrine.

"What did you say back at the hospital about self-absorbed people?"

"Okay, okay. You know I'm kidding, right?"

"Yes, Virgile. I know you're kidding."

Seeing that the apartment was too dark, Virgile opened the living-room shades, exposing the disgraceful fountain of the Three Graces that obscured the limited view of the Garonne River.

Alexandrine got out of her chair to look at herself in the mirror. Her smile vanished. Touching her cheeks and forehead, she collapsed in tears.

Spontaneously, Virgile went to her and wrapped her in his arms, just as he would his little sister. His cheek brushed Alexandrine's hair, and he smelled her perfume. He felt her chest heave with each sob. The woman curled against him was crying out for tenderness, and Virgile smoothed her hair, not daring to touch her battered face. But as he did this, he could sense his feelings change. She was no longer a little sister. He would have been embarrassed, but Alexandrine's need for comfort was more important than anything else. He kept smoothing her hair while rocking her gently.

Eventually she stopped crying, and her breathing became even. Virgile gently pulled away.

"I have nothing but wine to offer you," he said, getting up.

"The doctors advised me not to drink alcohol. I'm on an antidepressant, and the two don't mix."

"I might have a little orange juice. Let me check." Virgile was relieved to put a little distance between himself and the woman who was arousing unexpected feelings. He headed to the kitchen and opened the refrigerator door. "I lied. I only have tomato juice."

"That's fine."

He returned to the living room with the tomato juice, a bottle of Listrac—a Château Lestage—and two glasses. He filled the glasses.

"Virgile, I need to ask you for something."

"If it's in my power, it will be my pleasure."

"I may need more time before I can go home. Can I stay here until I feel better?"

Virgile nearly choked and rushed into the kitchen to drink a glass of water. He had been thinking only in terms of a day—maybe two at the most. He really hadn't thought it through. Of course she needed to stay in a place where she felt safe. Of course she could stay here. He'd sleep on the sofa, and she could take the bed. They'd make do.

When he came back to the living room, Alexandrine was standing at the window, watching the storm shoot bolts of lightning well beyond

Bouliac. She opened the window to feel the warm breath of the downpour.

"Thank you, Virgile. I always knew I could count on you," she said softly without turning around.

The wind was blowing the rain into the room, drenching Alexandrine's face like so many tears. Virgile walked up behind her and, during a clap of thunder, kissed her tenderly on the neck.

24

A lime-green Trabant with a battered fender and a dilapidated bumper was waiting for them in front of the inn. Zoltán was showboating at the wheel. His cousin Pavel was sitting next to him, laughing. Evidently Vilmos was a no-show. Perhaps he had stayed behind in the vineyards? At this time of year there was plenty of work to do.

Above the River Tisza, the sun had given way to thick charcoal-gray clouds driven by winds from the Russian plains. The air was more breathable now, much to Elisabeth's delight. She unbuttoned the collar of her silk blouse.

The backseat clearly didn't have enough room for both couples. But as it happened, Consuela was tired. More to the point, she was drunk and therefore excused from any visit. Benjamin wouldn't have minded taking a nap himself. There wasn't enough time, though, and Zoltán made it clear that he had arranged everything with his relatives.

Pavel didn't look much older than his cousin, but they hardly resembled each other. Pavel had coal-gray eyes, cropped chestnut hair, a handshake that could reduce a person's fingers to crushed grapes, and rather crude mannerisms. While Zoltán was hardy and cheerful, his cousin seemed clumsy and nondescript, even simpleminded.

The Cookers and Claude packed themselves into the backseat of the Trabant, which had most likely come off the assembly line when Leonid Brezhnev ruled with an iron fist. Benjamin wondered if that was being too generous. For all he knew, the car had been put together during the Khrushchev era. The winemaker had to give credit to the person who was keeping this jalopy on the road.

They were heading toward Mád. Vilmos was waiting for them there. So said Zoltán and Pavel.

When they arrived, a wrought-iron gate designed to go up and down like the entrance to a castle barred their access to the cellar. A gate as impressive as the wines themselves, Benjamin mused, thinking about the five hundred years of winemaking in this region.

Vilmos was holding the keys. A well-built man with thick eyebrows and darting light-colored eyes, Vilmos didn't resemble either his brother or Zoltán. It was hard to read into his gestures and intermittent smiles. He exuded something that could be interpreted as either distrust or deviousness.

"If these guys are cousins, I'll eat my hat," Claude said, mopping his brow with a handkerchief.

The wine cellar was built into a hillside and was almost undetectable from a distance. The visitors had to climb a steep path to reach the entrance. It resembled that of a chapel, with climbing roses clinging to the frame of the Romanesque door. Benjamin saluted the work of the builders of old. It was part of a huge subterranean labyrinth originally dug out to defend against Turkish invaders.

Elisabeth stopped in her tracks after Vilmos gave two turns of the key and opened the way into the dark tomb.

"What's wrong, darling?"

"Benjamin, I can't go in. I'm feeling claustrophobic." Elisabeth's breathing had changed, and she was leaning against the entrance.

"You have nothing to worry about, sweetheart. It's all well ventilated, and for the most part, the tunnels are wide. Remember the cellars in Champagne? It's the same idea."

"I have a bad feeling about this. Maybe I should have stayed behind, like Consuela. My head's spinning."

"Take a few deep breaths," Claude said.

"Let's just go on in. The coolness will do you good." Benjamin's words came out sharper than he had intended. Unlike his wife, he was eager to see the cellars.

Elisabeth closed her eyes for a moment and took a deep breath. "Okay," she said, opening her eyes again. "Let's go."

When everyone had descended the stairway leading to the dirt floor, Pavel turned on a string of bulbs that threw puddles of bluish light on rows of 140-liter casks lining the walls. The glass bungs atop each cask gleamed in the light.

The cellar was actually a tunnel cut right through the volcanic rock, with passageways on either side. Dark fungus carpeted the walls. Elisabeth reached out and touched it.

"Feel it, Benjamin. It's as soft as a rabbit's ears."

"It's like the *Baudoinia compniacensis* black mold in the Cognac wine warehouses, dear. The wine feeds the fungus as it evaporates. That's the angel's share. But first, before the wine ever gets here, the grapes are crushed into a syrupy aszú paste and mixed with a base wine that has already fermented in steel vats. The idea is to extract the natural sugars and aromas. Only then does it come here for a second fermentation, which could last years. Isn't that right?"

Benjamin turned to Vilmos and Pavel for an answer. They said nothing and just looked at Zoltán.

"Yes, yes. Aszú wine must age at least three years."

Zoltán pointed out that the humidity was nearly ninety percent, and the temperature was no higher than eleven degrees Celsius.

"Tell me, Zoltán, why are these wine casks called *göncs*?" Benjamin asked as he surveyed the walnut-stained barrels arranged in neat rows. The vintage and parcel were chalked on each one.

"Actually, they're called Gönci." Zoltán responded. "Gönc is a town in the Zemplén Mountains that's famous for its coopers. Even casks that don't come from there get the name now."

Benjamin lifted one of the glass bungs and listened to the Tokaji. It was fermenting. He invited Claude to lend an ear.

"Listen to the wine sing," he said. "It's always the same refrain, but I never get tired of it."

Vilmos picked up a glass pipette. He dipped the tool into the cask and inhaled until the pipette took on an amber color. Then he filled three glasses, the first of which he handed to Elisabeth.

Elisabeth shook her head, and Benjamin saw that she was shivering.

"Just a sip, sweetheart," he said. "It's not every day that we can have an experience like this."

She acquiesced and took the glass. But no sooner had she lifted it to her lips than she fell to the floor, dropping the glass and spilling the wine.

25

The broken slats of the shutters in the Rue Saint Rémi apartment were doing a poor job of filtering the brilliant sunshine. A large swath of Alexandrine's back was bathed in light. Only the sheet kept it from creeping below her tailbone.

Captivated, Virgile gazed at this lovely body dotted with beauty marks. Her skin had a musky sweet smell. It was silky and slightly tanned.

He would have to answer to his boss for taking the afternoon off, but at this moment all he could think about was the feel of pearly buttons under his fingertips, the awkward fumbling of zippers and shoelaces, the urgent dance to the bed, the surreal moment of this fantasy come true, and finally moaning and quivering bodies and feverish lips.

Virgile ran his fingers over the deliciously scented skin. Alexandrine turned over. Her eyes still closed, she drew her body close and nestled against his chest.

Alexandrine was working up to a passionate replay. Virgile was careful not to disturb the bandage on her nose or the stitches on her brow. He kissed her tenderly many times over, still astonished that they had actually made love after all the years she had refused his advances.

"For a woman who prefers women, you could have fooled me," he said between kisses.

"Don't make me laugh, Virgile. It'll hurt too much."

"Just so I get the full scope of what's just happened, you've got to tell me: white, rosé, or red?"

Alexandrine looked at him blankly. "I told you, I can't drink right now."

"No, let's say white for girls only—usually, at least, rosé for flexible from time to time, or red, for all-in bi?"

She looked into his eyes. "That's stretching the wine metaphor a bit far, even for you. And you know that's no question to ask a lady. What is it you really want to know? Would you be surprised if I said you're not the first man in my life?"

"Anybody I'd know?"

Alexandrine sat up and pulled the sheet over her breasts. She smiled, but Virgile could tell it was forced.

"There was a second-cousin. His name was Raphaël. I was in love with him when I was fifteen. We had a little fling one summer in Cap Ferret. Just a flirtation. Very innocent. He's married now to a girl from the Chartrons, a preachy sort who teaches catechism and leads the choir in a town in Gers, where he was just elected mayor. You know the type."

"Was he handsome?"

"I loved his blue eyes and his ass. So firm and round."

"So you're an ass woman," Virgile said, rolling over. "How does mine stack up?"

"No worries in that department. I've been ogling your posterior for a long time, Mr. Lanssien."

"Really, now? So what took you so long? You didn't have to go get beat up to hop in the sack with me."

Alexandrine's face went slack. She looked down and wrapped her arms around her knees.

"Oh, shit. I didn't mean that, Alex. But now that I've mentioned it, are you going to tell me what really happened to you?"

"It's complicated. I don't know if I can. Someday, maybe."

26

"**G**ood grief!" Benjamin cried out, patting Elisabeth's cheeks to revive her. "She's fainted."

A few seconds later, Elisabeth came to. "I'm fine, Benjamin." In truth, she looked pale and weak. "I just need some air."

"It's the black angels," Zoltán muttered. He told his cousin to help her out of the cellar. "In this maze she'll never find her way."

"Let me go with you," Benjamin said.

But Elisabeth refused his help. "Have your tasting. You've been looking forward to it." She took Pavel's arm, and the two started heading toward the entrance.

Benjamin knew that Elisabeth would be fine once she was outside and breathing fresh air. He felt guilty for insisting that she come along. "All right, let's get on with it," he told his tour leaders.

Benjamin picked up his glass again, giving it the respect it deserved. The *gönci* barrels were never subjected to unnecessary intrusions. They were virtual safes, where the wine aged for as long as eight years. Here, the Tokaji was precious as gold.

Benjamin sniffed and inspected the wine and then carefully chewed his first sip while Vilmos and Zoltán watched. A second later, the cellar went black.

The winemaker heard Vilmos call out to his brother. No response. Vilmos barked Pavel's name again. Still, nothing.

"No panic," he heard Zoltán yell. "He must be out by now."

Benjamin was wondering if he could feel his way out of the cellar, but he decided against it. Two steps, and he'd be walking straight into a wall. Better to let his guides figure out what to do. Surely this wasn't the first time they had lost their electricity.

He felt someone patting him. "Are we all here?" he heard Zoltán ask.

Two seconds later he heard the flick of a lighter, and the cellar took on an eerie glow. Benjamin looked around. For the first time he noticed a passageway filled with bottles wrapped in black crepe. Their golden caps stood out in the fu-nereal ambiance.

Zoltán lit a candle, which he handed to Vilmos. The cousin propped it in a glass next to Benjamin's and Claude's. The winemaker noted how the flame highlighted the amber color of the exceptional aszú. Then he glanced at Claude. In the candlelight his solemn face resembled a subject in a Maurice Quentin de La Tour painting.

But where was Pavel? By now, he should have been back.

"I'm worried about Elisabeth," Benjamin said. "She might have fainted again. We should make our way out of here."

"I'm sure she's fine," Zoltán said. "She just needed fresh air. We shouldn't miss this. Who knows if we'll ever return?"

Vilmos suggested they taste a new cask. Benjamin didn't need much coaxing. Indeed, when would he have this opportunity again? It was an older vintage, perfectly syrupy, with tones of apricot and mango and a hint of gingerbread.

Concentrating, Benjamin clicked his tongue against his palate three times to assess the aszú. He swallowed. Benjamin closed his eyes, as if he were communing with an unseen force, and said nothing. How could such bliss be expressed in mere words?

Finally, he spoke. "Silky and sweet. Luscious."

As Zoltán and Vilmos looked on, Claude imitated the winemaker's act of devotion. "Yes," he said. "A fine balance of fruit, acidity, and residual sugar."

"It's like Sauternes."

At that moment the electricity came on again. An orangish light illuminated the men and the casks. With a bright smile that displayed his perfect teeth, Zoltán greeted the return of the lights. Benjamin took the opportunity to examine the dates chalked on the casks. Aszú wine was not made every year. Like French sweet wines, it depended on the quality of the harvest.

Vilmos seemed eager to end the tour. Benjamin figured there was nothing more to be gained, as far as their guide was concerned, unless he was ready to hand over a fistful of cash for a couple of bottles.

Just as they were turning around to leave, a whistle resonated in the cellar. A second whistle ricocheted off the walls ten seconds later. The electricity flickered again, and Vilmos encouraged his group to hurry toward the exit. As they picked up their pace, Zoltán told Benjamin and Claude that prolonged human presence could alter the Tokaji, the same way frescos on the walls of ancient grottos could be damaged if too many people breathed around them.

Benjamin harrumphed. He knew about Lascaux, the famous caves that had to be closed because the drawings had deteriorated, but he had never heard such twaddle about wine in a cellar. It didn't matter. He was ready to leave anyway. Emerging from the labyrinth, he blinked in the harsh daylight and mopped his forehead. He looked for Elisabeth. She was nowhere to be seen.

27

They both jumped at the knock at the door. Alexandrine threw off the sheets and hopped out of the bed. She grabbed her clothes.

"Shit! Is it one of your girlfriends, Virgile?" she said, hustling to get into her lace undergarments. She hastened to button her tailored white blouse and headed down the hall looking for her pants and boots.

"Alex, relax. I don't have a girlfriend right now. Why does everyone think I've got them coming and going all the time?" He slipped into his jeans and pulled on a polo shirt.

He joined Alexandrine in the living room. The knocking became insistent.

Virgile opened the door to find a rather harried-looking Didier standing on the threadbare red carpet in the narrow hallway that served as a landing. He had one hand on the flower-patterned wallpaper and was breathing hard, probably from running up the spiral stairs.

"Didier! What are you doing here?" Virgile stood in the doorway and put both hands up to block him from coming in.

"Look, it's about Alexandrine."

"What about Alexandrine? Just who do you think you are, anyway? First you hang around the lab to find out who we're working with. Then you sidle up to my boss and get him to ask you to fill in at Cooker & Co. As if going after my job weren't enough, now you're stalking my friend and colleague Alexandrine! Just stop. Stop it all. You're way out of line. For all I know, you're the one who beat her up!"

Didier's eyes looked like saucers. Virgile stared right back at him.

"Virgile." The soft voice came from behind him. "It's not what you think."

Alexandrine nudged Virgile out of the way. He stepped aside, not sure of what to say.

"Alex, I need to talk to you," Didier asked.

28

Benjamin looked over at Claude, who had put on his Panama hat and was brushing the fungus off his beige shirt. Then the winemaker scanned the vines that extended well into the distance. The countryside seemed abandoned by its actors. Were all the vintners napping at this hour of the afternoon? And where were Elisabeth and Pavel?

Vilmos turned the key in the large lock and dropped it into his pants pocket.

"We need to find Elisabeth," Benjamin said, turning to Zoltán.

"I'm sure she's fine, Mr. Cooker," Zoltán answered. "My cousin probably took her into town. She's sitting in the shade of an apple tree or maybe relaxing near the fountain. Or perhaps he's taken her to a café for a cool drink."

Claude tried joking to make him feel better. Maybe Pavel and Elisabeth had struck something up. Slavic men, after all, had a certain charm.

Benjamin wasn't amused. With a rising sense of urgency he started down the path to Mád. He heaved a sigh of relief when he spotted her. She was sitting in the grass under a fig tree. The color had returned to her cheeks. He waved, and Elisabeth, wearing a smile, waved back.

"I was worried about you," he said when he reached her. "Are you okay?"

"Yes, I'm fine. I just needed to get out of there, Benjamin. I'm concerned about Pavel. He went to the village to get some water, and I haven't seen him since. I don't know what happened to him—"

Vilmos interrupted them. "I have to leave you now," he said. "I must get back to work."

Zoltán and Vilmos exchanged a few words in Magyar and nodded.

Benjamin thanked Vilmos for allowing them to visit the paradise of buried aszú and offered to buy a few bottles. Vilmos told them that Zoltán would handle the arrangements. They shook hands, and Vilmos took off at a trot in the opposite direction of the town.

Elisabeth looked at her husband. "I'm tired, Benjamin. Let's go back to the inn. Consuela was right to forgo the tasting. I should have done the same thing. And we don't know if Pavel's returning. Maybe something came up in town."

Driving back to the inn, Zoltán was quiet behind the wheel of the old Trabant. Benjamin had told Elisabeth to sit in the front with their guide but now he wondered if that was a wise decision. The old jalopy jostled on the turns and was full

124

of rust. The floorboards were bare in spots. They could see potholes beneath their feet.

Benjamin and Claude discussed the Tokajis they had tasted. They agreed on everything, diverging only on the length of finish.

"In any case, we'll be able to tell people that we did a blind tasting of some excellent aszús," Claude joked.

"You can say that again," Benjamin replied.

Elisabeth turned around and smiled at the two men. "So, you gentlemen had quite an underground adventure, didn't you?" she said.

Just as Claude and Benjamin were finishing their blackout tale, Elisabeth put a hand to her shoulder bag. She patted it, and then, with an alarmed look, she unzipped the bag and started rummaging through it. The color drained from her face.

"What's the matter, sweetheart?" Benjamin asked.

"My passport and wallet in my travel pouch. They're gone!"

"What?" the winemaker shouted, realizing the trap they had fallen into. He felt inside his jacket pocket and was relieved to find his passport and the euros he had slipped inside the document.

"It was Pavel!" Elisabeth said. "How could I have been so stupid? I shouldn't have taken my eyes off him!"

"What the... Zoltán, it was you! It's been you all along," Claude yelled. He fell upon Zoltán, seizing him from behind and wrapping his arm around his throat. "Stop the car!"

Zoltán began to choke, but instead of stopping, he stepped on the accelerator.

Elisabeth grabbed the wheel and cried out. "Stop it! Please! He had nothing to do with it."

The Trabant rounded a bend and plowed on for another ten yards before coming to a stop. Paying Elisabeth no mind, Claude dragged Zoltán out of the car and threw him onto the hood.

"You little bastard, you're going to tell us where your so-called cousin is," Claude shouted. "He's going to answer to me!"

Claude's face was red, and his breathing was quick. Benjamin leaped out of the car and rushed over.

"First my passport, then you hit on my girlfriend, and now this!" Claude was making a fist.

"I did nothing," Zoltán protested. "How could you accuse me of such a thing?"

Benjamin intervened, grabbing his friend's shoulders. "Calm down, Claude."

"I know it's all connected. He's a crook!"

"Claude!" It was Elisabeth. "That's enough. Zoltán, come on. Take us to your cousin's house so we can work this out. There must be some explanation."

Claude relaxed his muscles, and Benjamin let him go. Zoltán straightened up. Benjamin was studying him.

"Vilmos isn't really a vintner's son, is he? Is that why he hurried off and disappeared into the fields? We weren't supposed to be in those cellars were we? That's why we rushed out when we heard those two whistles? What about in the dark, when you patted me to find where I was? Was that really to pick my pocket?"

Zoltán looked around. He was preparing to run, but Benjamin was angry. Tears were glistening in Elisabeth's eyes. She had been the boy's advocate, insisting that he serve as their guide from Budapest to Tokaj. Benjamin knew she was indignant not only because she had been robbed, but also because she had been duped.

Benjamin grabbed Zoltán before he could bolt. Claude seized the other arm. The winemaker was surprised that they could subdue Zoltán so easily. Maybe he had muscles, but he didn't seem to know anything about the martial arts. Apparently he was just a guy who spent time in the weight room.

"And now you're going to take us to your damned cousin's house," Benjamin ordered, pushing him toward the car door.

The young man looked sheepish and stammered, seemingly compliant. "Pavel's just a distant cousin. I don't know Vilmos."

Elisabeth walked over to the guide imprisoned in Benjamin and Claude's grip and slapped him hard.

29

Virgile opened the window to get some air in the room.

"Nice view," Didier said, pointing at the patch of the Garonne and the bits of statue.

"Buckle it, Didier," Virgile said, pulling up a stool to sit on and leaving the two-seater Ikea sofa to Alexandrine and Didier.

"Sit down, the two of you. I want some answers."

There was a long moment of silence. Didier gazed from one bare wall to another. Alexandrine stared at her hands, folded in her lap. Finally, she spoke. "Didier and I have known each other since we were kids, Virgile."

"Are you lovers?"

"I won't answer that question, Virgile."

"Whatever your relationship, how do I know he's not the one who hurt you? You were fighting last week at the lab—I saw you."

"We weren't fighting," Didier said.

"Then it was a heated argument."

"Didier and I disagreed on what he should do about the Blanchards."

"The Blanchards?"

Alexandrine and Didier looked at each other.

"Come on, out with it!"

"Jules and his wife, Marie-Claire, are trying to oust Florence from the château and the business. Jules has always blamed her for their parents' death. Don't ask me why. They were in a terrible car crash. Florence wasn't even there—thank God. Now he's found papers that prove she was adopted, and he's claiming that she's not a legal heir. An insult to anyone who's adopted, if you ask me."

Virgile had stood up and was pacing now.

"Wait, wait... How do you know all this, Didier?"

Alexandrine and Didier exchanged glances again.

"Virgile, he works for them," Alexandrine said.

"No, this is very personal. He wouldn't know that in his position. Come on, even Mr. Cooker doesn't know this. Didier, you're sleeping with Florence, aren't you?"

Didier didn't respond.

"It doesn't matter," Alexandrine said.

Virgile ran his hands through his hair and put them on his hips. "What were you arguing about?"

"He wants to get their relationship out in the open and fight for the château. I say that it's a family affair, and he should stay out of it."

129

"Okay, okay. Whatever. What I want to know, Didier, is why you were snooping around Alex's place yesterday. I saw you trying to get in. What were you doing?"

"I dropped by the hospital and she'd left. I thought she might be home. That's all. You know how they are at hospitals. They never tell you anything."

"So, why are you here now?"

"Well, I figured if she wasn't at home, she'd be with you—after all the time you've spent with her since she was hurt."

"How… how do you… Oh, never mind. Why do you need to see Alex? What's so urgent?"

Didier turned to Alexandrine.

"Alex, I saw your father outside your house."

The blood drained from Alexandrine's face.

30

Benjamin stared at his wife and let go. Zoltán saw his opportunity. He freed himself from Claude's hold and sprang into the vines. He was out of sight in a matter of seconds.

Below them a flock of partridges rose into the air, most likely disturbed from their plunder of the grapes by Zoltán's headlong dash toward town. It was useless to pursue him.

"At least I have the car keys," Benjamin muttered.

"Let's just hope the car has enough steam to get us back to town," Elisabeth said.

"If it's steam we need, I think you can supply it, sweetheart. Even considering what you let off when you slapped our tour guide, I'm sure you have more where that came from."

"You know me, Benjamin. I can only be pushed so far. And I can't believe I let myself be deceived by that boy."

"It happens to the best of us," Claude said, his face still red with anger. "Look at me."

And with that he kicked the door of the lime-green Trabant, adding one more dent to the jalopy.

Behind the steering wheel, the usually in-control Benjamin Cooker felt like he had no control whatsoever. Even when he pushed the brake to the floor, the car kept going, although in no particular direction. The engine was rattling, and he heard another alarming noise each time he shifted gears. The speedometer looked ready to fall off the dashboard. The gas gauge, meanwhile, was quivering so much, Benjamin feared they would run out of fuel at the next bend in the road. The winemaker grumbled. If only he had his Mercedes 280 SL convertible.

"So, Benjamin, we're having quite the adventure, aren't we?" said Claude, who was sitting next to him.

"If you're trying to humor me, it's not working," Benjamin answered, his eyes on the lookout for potholes. "Let's just hope we make it back to town. I'm counting on your navigational skills, my friend."

Elisabeth was brooding in the backseat. Benjamin didn't blame her. She had allowed herself to be taken in by Zoltán and his band of petty thieves. A young man with an angelic face had managed to charm her in a church, and she had even championed him. Benjamin knew she'd have a hard time forgiving herself.

Claude took out his phone, but he was unable to pull up a map.

"If only we had been smart enough to bring one," he said.

Like a magician, Benjamin reached into his jacket and pulled out a tourist brochure listing the best Tokaji wineries.

"Hurray!" Claude yelled. A second later he grabbed the seat. Benjamin was trying to negotiate a final turn into the village of Tarcal.

It took them fifteen minutes to get back to their inn. When they arrived, a black-and-white police car and an ambulance, its lights flashing, were parked in front. Two paramedics were coming out the door with an unmoving form on a gurney. Benjamin and Claude rushed out of the car. It was Consuela. Her eyes were closed, and drool was trickling from the corner of her mouth. One of the paramedics was holding an IV bag above her head. Claude tried to intervene, but the police officers held him back.

"She's with me!" he yelled desperately.

Benjamin looked for Elisabeth. She was standing by the Trabant, pale and clearly fatigued.

"This is all too much," she said.

"You need to lie down."

Benjamin put his arm around her and led her to the inn, passing the officers and the paramedics. By now the innkeeper had emerged, and she was suspiciously eyeing Claude.

As soon as they were in the lobby, Elisabeth turned to Benjamin and told him she'd be okay. "I can get myself to our room. Don't worry. Go out and help Claude. He needs you."

Benjamin kissed his wife's cheek and went outside. The innkeeper was waving her arms and talking to the officers. Benjamin didn't understand what she was saying, but then one of the officers demanded Claude's papers. He produced the emergency passport issued by the French embassy.

"This looks like a forged document to me," the officer said, handing it to his colleague.

"What are you talking about?" Claude was nearly hysterical. "My papers were stolen in Budapest. This has the seal of the French embassy."

"Sir, you're going to have to come with us."

Claude now looked bewildered. "Where have you taken Consuela?"

"The woman has been taken to the hospital. Now come with us."

Benjamin knew it wasn't the right time to mention how their tour guide, a native of this very area, had fleeced them. And for sure he wasn't going to mention the fact that they were driving the boy's car, which was most likely stolen. The situation was too thorny, and the officers were too obtuse to care about the truth. One thing at a time, the winemaker told himself. But what needed to be done first? Elisabeth was ill, Claude was on his way to the police station, and Consuela was being taken to the hospital.

The officers settled the matter. As they loaded Claude into the back of their car, which was only slightly newer than the clunker Benjamin had appropriated, the two lawmen ordered the winemaker to stay at the inn until they returned.

Benjamin nodded and said nothing. Arguing would serve no purpose.

"Hungary boils down to one nuisance after another," he muttered as he went inside to join Elisabeth.

31

"**H**e's not my father."
  Alexandrine stood up, walked slowly into Virgile's bedroom.

Didier was on his feet and walking to the door.

"Where are you going?" Virgile asked, looking down the hall and back to the front door.

"Virgile, she's going to need you," Didier said, letting himself out.

Virgile rushed into the room. He took Alexandrine's swollen face in his hands and held it gently. Her eyes were filling with tears. He didn't say anything and just kept looking at her, waiting… Finally Alexandrine began to sob, her cheek against his chest.

"Who was the man outside your apartment?"

"My stepfather. Daddy died when I was three. I have no memory of him, only pictures. He was a general in the army. A handsome man with dark eyes—as elegant as Cary Grant in those movies from the nineteen forties and fifties. That's the image that sticks with me. Mother didn't stay single very long. She latched onto a rich aristocrat who had a mansion in the city, a villa on the Arcachon Bay, and other properties all over Bordeaux. As soon as they were married my mother took charge of emptying his pockets."

"'A woman worries about the future until she gets a husband, while a man never worries about the future until he gets a wife.' It's a quote the boss likes. Don't hit me."

Virgile's clumsy attempt to lighten the mood elicited a half-smile from Alexandrine. "You're no stand-up comedian. That's for sure." She continued her story as Virgile wiped away her tears with the corner of the bedsheet.

"I trusted him with all my heart. When I was a kid, my stepfather would give me anything I wanted. He called me his princess. It's true: he spoiled me, spoiled me rotten, until the day when…"

What remained of the sun's rays was now splashing against the far wall of the bedroom and the parquet floor.

"It was a summer day. Mother was off at some charity auction, at the Folmonts, I think. I was reading in my room. He came in and sat down beside me on the bed. He started stroking my hair. But then he touched my breast and began saying things. He loved me. I was so sweet. There was no shame in what we were feeling for each other. And he didn't stop…"

"How awful for you."

"I was in shock, Virgile. I didn't know what to think. I loved him, but what he did wasn't right."

"Did he come into your room again?"

"Yes, two or three more times. I threatened to tell my mother, so he stopped. And he became more generous with me. He was trying to buy my silence, I'm sure."

"Do you hate him?"

"No, I can't say that. He's the man who raised me. He paid for my studies and supported me when I had my oenology internships in Australia and California. But I couldn't kiss him anymore. I couldn't trust him."

"I understand. What a jerk!"

"No, you don't understand. For a long time I blamed myself for what happened. I thought it was my fault. I had lured him away from my mother. And then I was angry with myself for not loving him the way I should have. He asked me many times to forgive him, to forget what he had done. But I couldn't."

"You never said anything to your mother?"

"I was too ashamed. And I'm sure she would have protected my stepfather. My mother never had anything but her own interests at heart."

"You never thought of reporting him to the police?"

"When it happened, I was too young. When I got a few years older, though, I really wanted to say something. But it was too late. I figured the police wouldn't do anything. And who else would I tell? I was afraid of what my mother would do. I was sure she would disown me. Ironically, she wound up disowning me anyway. She won't have anything to do with me."

Alexandrine broke down again. She was curled against Virgile and murmuring snippets of words. He felt the tension drain from her body and sensed that she was relieved now, free of her burden. He became more tender, but it was the tenderness of a big brother, rather than of a lover.

"Under those circumstances, I understand why you like women better than men."

Alexandrine pulled away and looked at Virgile.

"If only our sexuality could be explained so easily, Virgile. Sure, I have trust issues when it comes to men. I feel more comfortable with women, and I'm drawn to women sexually. But now you know that I also enjoy having sex with a guy, especially a good-looking one like you. In the end, do we need an explanation for everything?"

"No, I guess not."

32

When Virgile sat down to call Benjamin, he wondered how he was going to skirt the question of Alexandrine and whether he should tell his boss about the Blanchard family's saga. But the man who answered the phone sounded distracted and distant, hardly the focused and self-confident Benjamin Cooker, one of the world's best-known wine experts and student of human nature.

"What's going on, boss?"

"I don't have the time or energy to tell you the whole story, son. We're in an impossible mess. Elisabeth's passport and wallet have been stolen, and we've been victimized by a ring of identity thieves, one of whom just eluded us, leaving us with his rotten jalopy, which is certainly a stolen car. I haven't had the chance to cancel Elisabeth's credit cards yet. Claude's girlfriend has just been sent to the hospital. They found her unconscious in her hotel room. And to top it off, he's been hauled to the police station."

"Talk about a Hungarian rhapsody! I think I hear some wrong notes."

"You can say that again."

"What's wrong with Claude's girlfriend?"

"I'm not sure. The innkeeper said it was an alcoholic stupor, and she was found in her room with three dead soldiers."

"Three stiffs?"

"No, three empty bottles of Champagne."

"As if your bubble weren't already burst."

"You don't have to try so hard to be funny, son. I'm not in the mood."

"Surely she couldn't have drunk all three by herself. Claude won't be too happy if he finds out she had help. Anyway, what can I do for you, boss? I feel pretty powerless back here in Bordeaux."

"Don't worry. You have your hands full with Alexandrine and the work at the lab. By the way, how are things going? Is she out of the hospital?"

"Yes, she is."

"And?"

"And, well, let's just say she still needs some time to recuperate."

"Did she tell you anything more about her attacker?"

Virgile went silent. "Well, actually, no, she didn't. She told me some other things, but not that."

"Well, keep trying. And how are things with Didier?"

"Now, that, too, is full of surprises. He isn't who I thought he was. It turns out he might not be so bad after all."

"Pray tell."

"Let's just say that life at the Blanchard château isn't so serene. The family has some ghosts in its closet."

Virgile summarized the situation.

"Florence didn't seem at all troubled when I saw her. She's even tougher than I thought. No wonder I'm so fond of her."

"Well, she has Didier to provide moral support. Meanwhile, I hope you're thinking about saving your own skin. We have enough problems without the cops throwing you in the slammer for driving stolen property—a useless Trabant, no less. As for Alexandrine, she intends to get back to the lab as soon as she's up to it. She knows the work is piling up. By the way, we received the Blanchard samples. They're excellent!"

"Good, good," Benjamin said.

33

The sun had been beating down on Tokaj all day, and the heat had become stifling. Even with night approaching, the air was still hard to breathe. Separated from the Nithard-Chavez couple, Elisabeth and Benjamin dined alone under the arbor. In the small inn, the afternoon incident was the topic of much gossip, and Benjamin had cajoled the innkeeper into giving him more information.

Early in the afternoon two men had shown up, asking for Miss Chavez. They described her perfectly. They said they were friends of her traveling companion and had a gift for her. They showed the innkeeper a box. It seemed innocent enough, so she gave them the room number. Miss Chavez ordered Champagne, and they stayed for quite a while, making a ruckus. Then everything went quiet, and the two men sneaked out like thieves, nearly running when they got out of the hotel.

"It felt off to me," the innkeeper said. "So I went and knocked on the door. When nobody answered, I unlocked it and discovered Miss Chavez lying half-undressed on the bed. The place was a mess, and there was a line of powder on the coffee table."

Benjamin was telling Elisabeth what he had found out over the meal. But he didn't have an appetite and couldn't eat much of his stuffed pike, although it was perfectly fine. The bottle of szamorodni that accompanied the fish also went unappreciated. Elisabeth wasn't especially hungry either. She just picked at her overdressed chicken salad.

"So she was doing drugs and drinking with two strange men in her room," Elisabeth said. "Who is this tart Claude found? Clearly not who she says she is. And to think that I had almost started to like her."

"There's a lot we don't know, darling. Who were those men, for example? We know for sure, though, that they weren't Zoltán and Pavel, because they were with us."

"Unless Zoltán has a clone. I think I'll try some of this szamorodni after all."

"Perhaps they were two homegrown gigolos?" Benjamin asked.

"I don't think they were gigolos. No woman with a body like hers would be paying for sex."

"You have a point. Still, she doesn't seem to be too discerning when it comes to men, especially when she's had too much to drink. Remember the other night at the Budapest Astoria? She was practically straddling Zoltán at the bar."

Elisabeth sighed. "Poor Claude. She managed to pull the wool over his eyes."

"Don't go believing Claude is that naïve."

"You don't think those two men have anything to do with my passport and wallet being stolen, do you?"

"Probably not…"

"That's reassuring," Elisabeth said, wiping her mouth with her embroidered napkin.

"Unless she's in cahoots with them."

"Benjamin, you are totally paranoid."

"Right now, dear, a measure of paranoia seems to be in order."

The couple passed on dessert and just ordered coffee. Benjamin drew a Havana from his cigar case and fell silent. The evening had failed to usher in cooler air. A rainstorm would have been a blessing, he thought.

The Cookers retired, knowing the next day would be trying. It was imperative that they contact the French embassy and get an emergency passport for Elisabeth. She needed the documentation to get home.

But first they had to report the theft to the police and recount how Zoltán, with the help of some accomplices, had taken advantage of them from Budapest to Tokaj. They would also tell the police about the Trabant parked outside the inn. They would need an interpreter to make sure the Hungarian authorities understood the entire story.

Meanwhile, as far as they knew, Claude was still at the police station.

Unable to sleep because it was still too hot, Benjamin sat on the balcony of his room, smoking a cigar. Just as he began to study the Big Dipper a shooting star flashed across the celestial vault. He took it as a good sign.

Shortly before midnight, a police car pulled up to the inn. An officer got out and opened the rear door. When Claude stepped out, Benjamin rushed down to meet his friend.

"Two double whiskeys, please," he said to the innkeeper.

They ducked beneath the deserted arbor. Claude looked haggard. His shoulders sagged, and there were dark circles under his eyes.

"Benjamin, they treated me like a common criminal, until they ascertained that my papers were real. They asked a long list of questions about Consuela before taking me to the hospital in Sárospatak to see her—or rather to question her."

Claude paused and stared at the ice cube floating in the amber whiskey.

"It was a horrible place. The paint was peeling. The linoleum floors reeked of ammonia. The few nurses were overwhelmed. A man in one of the rooms kept crying out. I didn't know if he was in pain or was crazy. Probably both."

"Sounds like a hospital."

146

"Believe me, Benjamin. I'd pick a French hospital over this one any day. While we were waiting for Consuela to regain consciousness, the officers told me the buildings were former army barracks. The place was converted to a hospice at the beginning of the twentieth century and to an urgent-care facility when Hungary was liberated."

"What about Consuela?"

"Her doctor said they'd found cocaine and alcohol in her system. Apparently the cocaine offset any fatigue that she might have felt, and she wound up drinking more than she could handle. Fortunately, she didn't choke on any vomit or stop breathing. And her liver seems to be okay."

"Claude, does she usually do drugs?"

"Not with me. But I don't know. When I went into the room, she didn't say anything, not even hello. She just stared. But I swear, it almost looked like she was smirking. The cops and I just stood there and she didn't utter a word. It was as if she had lost the ability to speak."

"Do you think she has brain damage?"

"The doctor said it was a possibility," Claude said.

"So the cops left empty-handed," Benjamin said.

"As did I," Claude said with a sigh. He sipped his whiskey. "They're taking this matter very seriously."

He fished the ice cube out of the whiskey and tossed it on the ground. Then he emptied the glass in one gulp.

"Did you get the feeling that Consuela understood what you were saying?" Benjamin ventured.

"Do you want to know what I really think?" Claude answered, looking Benjamin in the eye. "She's faking aphasia. She's too ashamed of what she did. She's a proud woman, you know. She'd never confess to anything as embarrassing as that."

"And, my friend, 'some that smile have in their hearts, I fear, millions of mischiefs.' You have to face reality, Claude. The woman who's sharing your life is not who she claims to be—it's more than the alcohol and drugs."

"Okay, stop right there, Benjamin!"

"Claude, we're friends, and I don't think you're totally aware of your ravishing tango dancer's flaws."

"What do you mean?"

"Consuela wasn't alone while we were sipping Tokaji in the dark."

Benjamin told Claude about the two visitors who had come to Consuela's room.

Benjamin knew he was being harsh, and he felt a tinge of guilt. But his friend deserved far better than what he was getting from the pretentious and unfaithful woman now in the hospital.

Claude stood up, took his glass, and looked for one last drop of whiskey. It was hopelessly empty. Furious, he threw it to the ground.

34

First came the squeaking brakes, then the thud of metal against plastic, followed by hydraulics and scrunching. But Virgile didn't open his eyes until the smell of the garbage truck on the street below wafted through the open window.

"Dammit," he said, jumping up to close it.

Alexandrine mumbled something and turned over, covering herself with the white sheet.

Virgile tiptoed out of the room. In the kitchen, he dug out a package of Blue Mountain coffee beans he kept for special occasions. From the top shelf of the cupboard, he took down the electric coffee grinder. He looked around the tiny space and hesitated. Then he stuck the grinder in the refrigerator so the noise wouldn't wake Alexandrine.

Five minutes later, he was back in the bed with two steaming cups of freshly brewed java.

Alexandrine propped herself up on the bed and thanked Virgile with a smile. She held the cup with two hands and enjoyed the aroma.

"It's not free."

"What are you talking about?"

"Well, in exchange for this fine cup of the best coffee in the world, I would like you to tell me the whole truth."

Alexandrine's eyes went dark.

"You haven't actually told me what your step-father was doing at your place. Nor have you told me what actually happened the day you were attacked."

Alexandrine said nothing.

"Nobody is trying to reprimand you. I just want the name of the lout who hurt you."

Alexandrine sipped her coffee and closed her eyes as she savored the taste. She took a deep breath.

"The day it happened, Dadou showed up at my place. I know. It's a ridiculous nickname, but I've never been able to call him Papa or Dad. Actually, his name is André. You know that my family never wanted much to do with me after they found out I liked women. But Dadou would still show up every once in a while. He's a drunk. He was always three sheets to the wind when he came to my room. At first, he was never mean. That came later. I think he's beaten my mother a few times, but she'd never admit it, even to me."

"Perhaps especially to you," Virgile said.

"Anyway, he was drunk when he came to my apartment that day."

She set her cup of coffee down next to the bed and wrapped her arms around her knees.

"He said on the intercom that he had something important to tell me. Like a fool, I let him up. I should have known he was drinking. He came into the apartment and looked around. Then he saw a photo of Chloé on the mantel. 'Who's the slut?' he asked. I tried to distract him, but he wouldn't let it drop. He said he didn't like lesbians, that he was ashamed of his daughter and her depraved morals. I told him I wasn't his daughter and I never would be. Then he came at me, calling me a little bitch."

A single tear rolled down her cheek.

"At first he slapped me, and then he starting punching. Dadou's a big guy. He could break you into little pieces without much effort. The more I screamed, the more he hit. I started gushing blood. Then he got scared and ran off, threatening to kill me if I told anyone. You believe me, don't you?"

"Of course I believe you. God help the guy if I ever lay eyes on him. He won't know what hit him."

"Do you understand now why I don't want to go back to my apartment? The blood stains are still all over the place."

Once again Virgile took her in his arms. He stroked her hair and her back. Alexandrine had confessed the unspeakable. Her stepfather had stolen her virginity and her childhood dreams. And he had come back, haunting her like a ghost and beating her. Worse, he was still out there, lurking. If only she could move past this and find a semblance of peace.

The sun was already high in the Bordeaux sky when Alexandrine and Virgile abandoned the rumpled bed, where their lovemaking had unraveled Alexandrine's dark secrets. After a cool shower, they ventured out to the Place Camille Jullian and shared a late breakfast.

35

Reaching the French ambassador was no easy feat. Benjamin had tried the entire morning, but the ambassador had not deigned to answer his calls. The winemaker took this as a bad omen. Elisabeth was very worried, but Benjamin, grumpy and distracted, reminded her of the many obligations of a diplomat in charge of guaranteeing France's cultural prestige.

"Benjamin, stop patronizing me. I know very well what an ambassador does."

The winemaker knew better than to bicker. It would only make matters worse.

It was noon when the ambassador finally responded. The winemaker related the problem in detail.

"You've been having rotten luck, Mr. Cooker. It seems that you're the favored target of traffickers in identity papers, or else your naïveté attracts crooks like wasps to overripe fruit."

"So it appears," Benjamin replied tersely.

For honesty's sake, Benjamin felt obliged to tell the ambassador about the new problems his friend Claude was facing, the same Claude Nithard whose passport had found its way into questionable hands. The ambassador was both polite and curious.

"Mr. Ambassador. Would you be able to do me a favor?"

"Mr. Cooker, considering what you've been through, I would be delighted."

"Would you please find out if Consuela Chavez was truly born in La Plata, Argentina? I'm having some doubts about her identity."

"I'll check it out. In the meantime, I suggest that you inform the Tokaj police of all your troubles. Several identity-theft rings have been disbanded in Budapest, but it's clear that the crime is still flourishing. I'm going to request that an honorary consul from Zemplén help you. He'll do the interpreting and will be sure to get your version of the facts heard."

"Thank you, Mr. Ambassador. We were planning to contact the police, but I was concerned about getting our story across in full detail."

"I'm truly sorry, Mr. Cooker, that you've had all these troubles. But is it not true that rot sometimes gives rise to the best wines, like the Tokajis?"

"You have a point. Maybe some good can come of this. I can only hope," Benjamin said, thanking the diplomat again.

Claude Nithard had shut himself up in his hotel room. Benjamin suspected that he had considered taking a taxi to Sárospatak and demanding an accounting from Consuela. But that would have been fruitless. She wouldn't have talked. To deal with his humiliation and pain in private, he had given the winemaker the excuse of having to finish his manuscript. Sooty clouds were clinging to the Carpathian Mountains, and a few drops of rain were possible, but the heat had let up.

The honorary consul sent by the French ambassador, a Breton from Telgruc-sur-Mer, was meeting them at two thirty sharp in Tokaj.

"We can't be late," insisted Elisabeth, who was growing increasingly apprehensive. Although she didn't say anything, Benjamin knew she feared the police would detain them, the same way they had held Claude. Benjamin had to admit that he was a little nervous too.

At the appointed time and spot, the couple from Bordeaux made the acquaintance of Padrig Legarrec, a fiftyish man with graying temples. The honorary consul was sitting on the edge of a fountain that was in rather poor taste, a contemporary-looking Bacchus slumping over a wine barrel. He had lived in this part of Hungary for twenty-five years and had married a girl from Szegi. But he still missed France.

"Well, the ocean, in particular," he said.

At any rate, he was quite proud to be in the company of the author of the famous *Cooker Guide*. Legarrec claimed to be a layman, but his knowledge of Burgundy wines was considerable. Apparently, this Breton favored them.

Before they went to the police station, Benjamin related their epic once again, from Budapest to Tokaj. The man looked sympathetic, but didn't seem ready to believe that Elisabeth's passport had wound up in the hands of a gang trafficking in identity papers.

"These petty thefts—most of the time it's kids who just want the money," he said. "You know how they like their brand-name shoes."

The police station was shabby retro: a laminate desk, a tinplate lamp, an ancient computer with a tiny screen, and photographs of the Danube tacked to the whitewashed walls. Three officers were waiting for them, one of them the man who had placed Benjamin under house arrest the previous day. The officer gave the honorary counsel an icy greeting. The two exchanged a few comments in Magyar, and then the officer sat down at his old computer.

The winemaker carefully reconstructed his Hungarian adventure, his status as a man of the arts, his longstanding friendship with Claude Nithard, and his desire to know everything about aszú wines, which he placed in the pantheon of liqueurs.

Then he related their seemingly fortuitous meeting with Zoltán. The boy's eagerness to please had impressed his wife, and they had hired him to be their guide. But then the trip began to fall apart. There was the episode at the Gellért Baths, followed by Claude's misadventure, the bizarre tasting in the Tokaj cellar belonging to a wine-maker whose name he read on some labels but whose real son he was no longer sure he had met. As Legarrec methodically interpreted Benjamin's saga, the officer stopped the winemaker from time to time to ask questions and have him repeat certain facts. Elisabeth, meanwhile, was nodding to reinforce her husband's words.

The officer quit tapping on the keyboard and turned to the Breton intermediary.

"Please ask Mr. Cooker if he would be able to recognize the men who took him to the wine cellar."

"Certainly," the Cookers answered in unison when the interpreter finished asking the question.

The investigator opened his desk drawer and took out a dog-eared folder. He removed some black-and-white photos and slid them across the desk. Benjamin and Elisabeth studied the pictures for several minutes but didn't recognize anyone. The officer took another handful of pictures out of the folder and passed them over. Still, none of the faces looked familiar. Then Benjamin leaped from his chair.

"*That* one I know!"

Elisabeth looked at her husband with wide eyes.

"It's Viktor! He was on the ship with us, a crewmember, the one who plied us with beer the night Claude was in the doldrums. I recognize him perfectly. He even gave Claude his number. Too bad Claude threw it away. He was grilling us about our trip, the bastard. Now I understand. He was mapping his plans!"

For the first time, the Hungarian police officer broke into a smile. He handed Benjamin another photo.

"And this one was his sidekick," Benjamin said. "There's no doubt about it. His name was Attila. He was quieter than the other one. I should have known better. I didn't like his looks."

At the behest of the police officer, Legarrec asked Benjamin if he was sure.

"Absolutely sure," the winemaker replied.

The officer looked to Elisabeth for confirmation. She couldn't respond with the same certitude as her husband, but now she remembered the two men in the photos. They were definitely on the ship. To that she could attest.

The officer turned back to the computer and tapped away. With a satisfied expression, he finished typing and lit a cigarette. He exhaled the smoke and asked if Claude would confirm what the winemaker had just said.

"Yes, I'm sure he can," Benjamin answered.

The Hungarian officer and Legarrec then launched into a discussion that Benjamin couldn't follow. But the tone sounded full of innuendo, and Legarrec's face had suddenly clouded over.

"Mr. Legarrec, can you tell me what the officer just said to you?"

The Breton looked carefully at the officer and then turned to Benjamin.

"The two individuals you've just identified are precisely the ones who came to your hotel yesterday afternoon and asked for Mr. Nithard's companion."

"Oh, no," Elisabeth murmured.

Benjamin felt his throat tighten. He reached for his wife's hand and squeezed it. Then he withdrew a Bolivar cigar from his sharkskin case.

"May I?" he asked the officer, who was crushing his cigarette in an ashtray that was, in fact, a re-purposed shell casing.

"Be my guest," the officer answered.

The winemaker lit up his Cuban and took a long drag. He let the smoke calm him while he assimilated the news.

After a few moments Benjamin gave the Trabant keys to the guarantor of Hungarian security, whose demeanor had become relaxed. The officer asked the two French citizens to initial their statement. Then he leaned over to examine the ring of Benjamin's cigar.

"Imensas from Bolivar, seventeen centimeters long, impeccable draw," explained the *Cooker*

159

Guide author, as he pulled another one out and offered it to the officer. "Hints of coffee and honey. Please translate, Mr. Legarrec. Cigar smokers are always good company. It's true throughout old Europe. Spread the word."

After they filed their complaint, the Cookers, relieved but still perplexed, invited Padrig Legarrec to their inn for a glass of aszú. The Breton needed no convincing. Benjamin autographed the latest edition of his guide and gave it to him. Legarrec was flattered. As the discussion of the cost of aszú grapes wore on, Elisabeth excused herself.

"I'm going to check on Claude," she told Benjamin, who nodded and kissed her on the cheek.

Padrig Legarrec finally took his leave after a third glass of Tokaji, a lovely concentration of sweetness from a young winemaker named Zoltán Demeter. The two men praised the excellent aszú, but Benjamin found himself thinking about the treachery of his own Zoltán. Surely the young man had returned to Budapest, where, in urban anonymity, he was pursuing naïve tourists on some church steps or in markets rife with the aroma of paprika.

Benjamin returned to his room and found Elisabeth reading a book.

"I knocked on Claude's door, but he didn't answer. Then I checked with the innkeeper, and she said he had taken the taxi to Sárospatak. Maybe he'll be back by dinnertime."

Evening fell, and Claude Nithard did not materialize. Benjamin stayed up part of the night, waiting for him with an open cedar box of cigars and his notepad, where he jotted down some thoughts on the Tokajis he had tasted during the trip. Still, Claude didn't show up. The shutters in his room were closed and latched. And yet Benjamin could make out his friend's Panama hat hanging from the lever.

36

Virgile had left Alexandrine with a stack of wine magazines and returned to Cooker & Co. to look over the lab reports that were coming in. The situation there was improving.

At the end of the day, he returned to the apartment to find Didier and Alexandrine setting the table.

"Virgile, I hope you don't mind. I invited Didier over."

"I picked us up something to eat," Didier said, with his signature grin.

Virgile set down his things. "I hope it's not pizza."

"Man of little faith. I went to that restaurant down the street and brought us some foie gras with fig jam and, just for you, son of Bergerac, some *magret de canard*. I'm presuming you'll have a decent bottle to serve up."

Virgile took in the spread of food and the relaxed look on Alexandrine's face. Her nose was still bandaged, but Virgile couldn't miss the light that had come into her eyes again. Was it because

Didier was there? Virgile felt the usual jealousy bubbling up again and reminded himself that Didier was not actually his rival. So maybe that glimmer in Alexandrine's eye was from their romp under the sheets?

"Alex, you're looking so much better. That bandage will be coming off in no time."

"I guess confession is good for the soul and the body," Alexandrine answered, smiling. "I've kept that secret for too long. I think I'm beginning to turn the corner."

Virgile grabbed a set of keys from a wall hook. "I'll go get us a bottle from the cellar. Something classic for duck?"

"No Médoc—we get that all the time, or Fronton, which goes best when the duck is served with spices," Didier said.

"Well, what about a wine from my home region then, a Bergerac? I've got a few older bottles with smooth tannins that will be just right. I'll grab a Graves too for the foie gras."

The three of them sat around the table, spreading foie gras on toast. Didier and Virgile sipped wine, while Alexandrine stuck to water. Virgile filled them in on Mr. Cooker's misadventures in Hungary.

Virgile got up to heat up the main course and grab the second bottle of wine, which he had opened earlier to allow it to breathe.

"You're not really heating the duck in the micro-wave, are you?" Didier said.

"Don't worry, I got it!" Virgile said, bringing the dish to the table and serving up the red wine. They started in on the main course.

"I'm not used to being so idle," Alexandrine said. "Tell me about your day."

"We're catching up on lab reports. How are things on the mildew front, Didier?"

"On the list of vintners you gave to me, only one said he hadn't found any mildew in his vine-yard. I told him he probably hadn't looked close-ly enough, considering the high humidity and the temperatures."

"Good answer. You should stop by tomorrow and give the vines a good look. How'd you get on with that newbie vintner? The idealist from Paris who thinks he can make wine without treating the vines at all?"

"I told him he should do the canopy manage-ment himself, and after he spent a full day of pick-ing off leaves to give the bunches some sunlight, I went back and he was nearly begging me for some effective treatment. We agreed on dusting sulfur."

"That's organic at least."

"Boys, you've got to stop. I want to go back to work so much. Enough, I want to get back to my normal life," Alexandrine cut in.

Both men looked at her and an uncomfortable silence followed.

"What?"

Didier was the first to speak up. "You can't just let it be with your stepdad."

"He's right, Alex. You've got to report him."

She set down her knife and fork. "What's past is past."

"Listen, Alex, your childhood is one thing, but the man attacked you in your home. He's dangerous. The only way you're going to come to any peace and be able to go home and, as you say, get back to a normal life, is to get him locked up."

She stood up and walked over to the window.

"Virgile's right," Didier said. "It's like with the Blanchards—when you keep the ghosts locked away in silence, they always find a way to come back and haunt you. You've got to talk about it. You've got to get this out in the open."

Virgile walked over to her, put his hands on her shoulders, and turned her around. "Alex, Mr. Cooker has connections with the police. We can go see Inspector Barbaroux together, okay?"

She looked him in the eye, then looked at Didier. "Okay, okay, you win."

Then she grinned. "I see you've already bonded in a conspiracy against me."

37

The following day, Benjamin knocked again on his friend's door, without success.

"I'm worried," Elisabeth said when he came back to their room.

Benjamin only nodded in response.

An overnight rainfall had vanquished the suffocating heat that had assaulted Bald Mountain for three days. Ribbons of mist were floating like bridal garlands above the vines. The air, swept in by a capricious cool breeze, was finally breathable. But Benjamin paid it no mind. He paced the balcony. Claude had turned off his cell phone—or had he let it die? Benjamin tried to calm himself. Claude often ignored his phone. The fact that it wasn't working didn't mean anything.

He was about to go to the Tokaj police station to report the disappearance of the renowned Parisian publisher. But just as he was extinguishing his cigar, a large black sedan with tinted windows pulled up to the inn. The driver stepped out and hastened to open the door for the passenger in the backseat.

The slender silhouette of a distinguished-looking man emerged from the car. He had a tanned face and wavy hair, and he was carrying a leather briefcase. He hurried into the lobby of the little inn, his chauffeur on his heels. Apparently, the driver was also his bodyguard.

To Benjamin, who was watching from his balcony, it looked like a scene from a Gilbert and Sullivan operetta.

The phone in the room rang, and Benjamin, went back in to pick it up. The innkeeper informed him deferentially that the French ambassador was waiting for the Cookers in the lobby. Benjamin took care to button his collar and smooth his hair before taking his wife's hand and joining the emissary of the French government.

"Benjamin Cooker!" exclaimed the representative of the foreign ministry.

"Mr. Ambassador," the winemaker replied, a bit embarrassed by the exuberant greeting.

"It's a pleasure," said the ambassador, clearly delighted to be rubbing shoulders with a French national whose reputation in winemaking spanned the globe.

"The pleasure is ours, sir. Let me introduce my wife, Elisabeth."

As the hulking driver looked on, the three shook hands.

"I wanted to personally deliver your emergency passport, Mrs. Cooker," the ambassador said. "I'm sure the document will ease your concerns in regard to the Hungarian authorities. You should be able to travel with no problems whatsoever. But I also came to discuss one particular aspect of this situation..."

"Yes?" said the winemaker.

"I should say a more unfortunate aspect."

"Meaning?"

"It's about your friend, Claude Nithard. More precisely, it's about the person he brought with him. Your hunch was right, Mr. Cooker. This woman has been known by the Hungarian police for a few years now."

"How is that?" asked Benjamin.

The ambassador ushered the Cookers out to the garden, telling his chauffeur with a nod to stay behind. They began to stroll along a gravel path lined with pink carnations, gentians, and asclepias.

"Mr. and Mrs. Cooker, Consuela Chavez has, shall we say, a scandalous past."

"What do you mean by that?" Benjamin asked.

"Let me be clear. This woman is about as South American as I'm Neapolitan. Her family is Eastern European. Actually, they're gypsies. Consuela's grandparents fled the Nazi regime when Himmler ordered a census of the gypsies. In doing that, they managed to avoid the extermination camps."

Benjamin slowed down and looked at the diplomat, waiting for the moment of truth.

"They tried to get to the United States, but they were penniless, so the family settled in the south of France, in Nîmes, and then in Toulouse."

"I knew it," Elisabeth said. "I told you she had a Toulouse accent."

"As I said, they had no money. Consuela's mother was born into poverty. When she was no more than a teenager, she got pregnant and gave birth to Consuela. Her parents had thrown her out, and the baby's father was never in the picture. As a child, Consuela was neglected—her mother was either drinking or turning tricks, and in time, Consuela was turning tricks herself in a seedy hotel near the Matabiau train station. She left her traces in Cannes, too, and then Nice. Her one passion was tango dancing. She frequented the clubs and became quite good at it."

"Yes, that's how she met Claude."

"That was when she put herself under the protection of some unscrupulous Hungarians from Prague and Budapest. Time and again she was taken into custody on suspicion of prostitution, petty theft, or trafficking in false papers. But she was always released for lack of evidence."

Benjamin remained silent. He was thinking of Claude, madly in love with the gorgeous brunette who had set his *corazón* on fire.

Sad for his friend, the winemaker sighed. "We had our doubts. There was something about her that didn't add up. But it's quite a leap to imagine all of this."

"I haven't finished," the ambassador said. "Now we come to Viktor and Attila, the men you met on the Danube. It seems they were buddies with Consuela's protectors. Viktor and Attila run a nice little business stealing wallets, credit cards, passports, and the like. It got even nicer when all hell broke loose in Syria, and Syrians with money began to look for safe ways to make it to Europe. They were willing to pay for doctored French passports, and Viktor and Attila were more than happy to meet the demand."

An ancient Buddhist monk's quote came to Benjamin. "'The human mind, with its infinite afflictions, passions, and evils, is rooted in the three poisons: greed, anger, and delusion.'"

"Yes, they made a lot of money on the suffering of those people," the diplomat said. "Human nature can be quite base."

"Was Consuela in on the thefts?" Elisabeth asked. "Did she plan to fleece us from the start?"

"We don't believe she had anything to do with the theft of your passport and wallet or with Mr. Nithard's. Our intelligence says they haven't been in contact for a long time. We picked up Viktor and Attila, and they swear they paid her a visit because they knew her, that's all. They recognized her on the boat."

"What about Zoltán? Is he connected to Viktor and Attila?" Elisabeth asked.

"A known associate. Zoltán and his accomplices were responsible for the thefts, but they were just underlings. It's a surprise to find him so far from Budapest, though. Until now, the authorities thought he was just hanging out around the basilica."

"He's an opportunist, and a good one." It was Elisabeth again. "Do you think he stole Claude's passport?"

"He probably had a hand in it, but the ringleaders were Viktor and Attila, who are in custody now. They're charged with engaging in organized crime and homicide."

Elisabeth gasped and looked at Benjamin.

"Homicide?" Benjamin asked.

"It seems Interpol had an agent tailing them. He was posing as an artist."

"Connor was a spook? Well, what do you know? We met him on the ship. We heard that he met with an unfortunate end. I never would have guessed the incidents were connected."

"We found his body near the St. Stephen's Basilica in Budapest. He had been shot."

Benjamin didn't know how much more news he could take. "He said he was trying to get his fiancée out of Syria."

"That was the story he was using to infiltrate the paper-trafficking ring. Those two thugs will pay dearly for his death."

The ambassador reached into his jacket and pulled out a leather cigar case. It contained two maduro-wrapped cigars with perfectly oiled caps.

"You smoke cigars, Mr. Ambassador?" Benjamin asked.

"It's a habit I picked up during my first diplomatic assignment. I was the French ambassador to Honduras. In that country, how could you resist a puro? There are no vineyards in Honduras, but the country has its finer points. Would you do me the pleasure of having one with me?"

Benjamin accepted the cigar and took out his cutter. He sliced the top from his Havana and handed the highly specialized accessory to the ambassador, who did likewise, with perhaps a little less elegance.

When Benjamin raised his eyes to savor the first puff of his cigar, with its impeccable cap and aromas of wool and bitter oranges, he noticed that the window in Claude's room was finally open. The Panama hat was no longer hanging from the shutter.

38

Claude had chosen to fly back to Paris from Debrecen International Airport. He had work to tend to back home, and he had seen quite enough of Hungary.

Benjamin and Elisabeth, however, decided to extend their vacation a few more days. Virgile had gotten things under control at the lab. The estate owners had been appeased, and although the winemaker was eager to see Alexandrine, he couldn't do any more for her than what Virgile was already doing. Elisabeth insisted on taking the train back to Budapest and spending just a little more time in the city. After everything they had been through, he didn't have the heart to refuse her.

When they arrived in Budapest, the couple checked into the Astoria once again.

"So, what shall we do first, dear?" Benjamin asked after a light lunch of duck and sour cabbage strudel with a juniper and paprika sauce in the hotel's restaurant. "Fishermen's Bastion? The Great Synagogue?"

"Actually, Benjamin, I'd like to go back to the basilica."

The winemaker set down his cup of espresso. "Why do you want to go back there, my dear, with everything that's happened? I thought we were putting all our troubles behind us and giving ourselves a fresh start."

Elisabeth reached out and took her husband's hand. "I understand how you feel, Benjamin. But it's something I need to do. Ever since we talked with the ambassador in Tokaj, something hasn't seemed right. It's not settled yet, as far as I'm concerned. Maybe going back to the basilica won't answer my questions, but I still want to go."

Benjamin sighed. When his wife's mind was made up there was nothing he could do but go along.

"All right, sweetheart. We'll go to the basilica."

Benjamin paid the bill, and Elisabeth took her husband's arm. The two headed toward the hotel entrance and, once outside, caught a cab.

"St. Stephen's Basilica," Benjamin told the driver.

"Ah, the monkey paw," the driver said. "Everyone who comes to Budapest has to see it."

Benjamin and Elisabeth didn't respond. A few minutes later they were standing in front of the basilica. They looked at each other and walked up the steps to the entrance. Inside, the basilica was filled with people—tourists, Benjamin assumed. A large group was crowded around the exhibit with the hand. The winemaker took the opportunity to admire the basilica's neo-classical architecture. He wished they had timed their visit better, because he would have loved hearing the six bells, five in the left tower and one in the right.

Just as he was turning to tell his wife about the organ concerts in this place of worship, something caught his eye. He looked to his left, and there was Zoltán, in his jogging suit and athletic shoes. The boy with the angelic face was staring at the group gathered around the hand. No doubt that he was getting ready to pounce on his prey.

Benjamin tapped Elisabeth's arm and nodded in Zoltán's direction. He wanted to leave and contact the authorities. The boy hadn't spotted them yet. But before he could say anything, Elisabeth bolted off toward Zoltán. Benjamin was frozen in his tracks. This was a matter for the police to handle, not them. A second later, the winemaker came to his senses and rushed after his wife. If he couldn't stop her, at least he could protect her.

"What, in God's name, is she thinking?" he muttered, trying to catch up.

Zoltán turned away from the crowd and locked eyes with Benjamin. He grinned.

"Mr. and Mrs. Cooker," he said when they finally reached him. "What a surprise. I never expected to see you here again."

"I bet you didn't, Zoltán," Elisabeth said. "So, you're scouting your next victims? I bet those tourists over there would like to know what you're up to."

Zoltán gave Elisabeth a wide-eyed look and put his hands in the pockets of his jogging suit. "I don't know what you mean, Mrs. Cooker. I'm a tour guide. You know that."

Benjamin was keeping a close eye on his wife. She was staring angrily at Zoltán, and whenever Elisabeth gave him that look—which wasn't often—Benjamin knew it was best to watch his step.

"You can act innocent with other people, young man, but not with me," Elisabeth pressed on. "We know what you did, and it wasn't just stealing wallets and passports, was it? The police have charged your two bosses, Viktor and Attila, with murder, but something about that doesn't add up."

Elisabeth had backed Zoltán against one of the stone walls.

"What were they actually doing in Tokaj? They didn't go just to see Consuela, did they? Old friends, my foot. They came after you, didn't they?"

She was sticking a finger in his chest now. Zoltán seemed too surprised to even answer.

"They didn't kill that artist, did they? He never approached them for the French passport he needed for his fiancée. He approached you. That's why you disappeared when we saw him in front of the church. This was your chance to make more money than you were getting from your bosses. You usually handed the stolen passports over to them. But now you saw your opportunity to be a direct provider."

Zoltán was fidgeting now. Nerves were getting the better of Benjamin too. He scanned the crowd. Would the boy dare to do anything to them with that many onlookers? And what about Elisabeth? What was she capable of?

"Okay, okay," Zoltán said, clearly trying to appease Elisabeth. "A guy like me has a hard time finding a job these days. So I take money and passports from rich people. No big deal. They can afford it."

Elisabeth wasn't going to let up.

"But it is a big deal now, Zoltán, because you crossed the line. You began to get nervous about that artist when you discovered that he had drawn you. And you figured he wasn't who he said he was. Well, he wasn't. He was an undercover agent. You didn't care who he was working for. You needed to be rid of him. And you lost your head, didn't you, Zoltán? You shot him with a gun one of your buddies had gotten on the black market."

Now panic was written all over Zoltán's face. He turned and lunged toward the entrance. Without thinking, Benjamin reached out and tried to stop him, but he was too late to grab his arm. At that moment, Elisabeth stuck her leg out. Zoltán tripped and fell to the stone floor, face down. Benjamin pounced on him. Blood was spilling from his forehead, but he would live. By that time, the crowd had gathered around the couple and their captive.

"One of you, please call the police," Elisabeth called out to the onlookers. Benjamin couldn't believe what he had just witnessed. But then, he had never sold his wife short.

Elisabeth stood over the boy she had trusted, the boy who, overnight, had gone from petty thief to murderer. Zoltán struggled to turn over and look at her. She planted her black sling-back low-heel pump on his neck to keep him still.

"'If you will forgive me for being personal,'" she said, looking down at him. "'I do not like your face.'"

She turned to Benjamin and grinned. "You're not the only one who can remember quotes, honey. Agatha Christie, *Murder on the Orient Express*."

Epilogue

After a heat wave in July, the weather through-out Médoc was rainy and windy. Finally, at the end of summer, the storms gave way to brilliant skies. In Listrac, the harvest took place under a vermillion sun. Full of sugar, the grapes were healthy and abundant. The Blanchard family's vats were quickly full.

The family's legal issues, however, clouded Florence's days. She managed to keep her chin up through the whole process, even when Didier moved on to someone else, and she won the case. Florence didn't lose her château or her stake in the business. And Jules eventually decided to sell her his interest.

Inspector Barbaroux, by order of the examining magistrate of Bordeaux, brought Alexandrine de La Palussière's stepfather in for questioning on suspicion of assault. Because Alexandrine would have had to press charges years earlier, the man couldn't be charged with rape. Still, he faced the prospect of a long prison sentence, and

Alexandrine was feeling vindicated. After questioning, her stepfather drove out to his property in Latresne, cleaned one of his hunting rifles, and shot himself in the head.

Chloé reappeared, and Alexandrine parted ways with Virgile. It was better, after all, to keep their relationship on a professional level. Virgile wasn't too heartbroken, as he was still smitten with Margaux Cooker and probably always would be. But she was in New York, and he was sure Mr. Cooker would never allow it. Virgile consoled himself with a young Chilean hired for the Mouton-Rothschild harvest.

That year's *Cooker Guide* surpassed all expectations. Some five hundred thousand copies were sold, and it was published in seventeen languages. This was hardly the only bright spot in Claude Nithard's life. One of his writing protégés won the Renaudot Prize, and his daughter, Anaïs, granted him the status of grandfather with the birth of a boy. She had considered naming him Victor, but the new grandfather persuaded her to choose another name.

For his part, the Bordeaux winemaker added the French ambassador to Hungary to the list of friends he cultivated over vintage bottles of wine and cigars. During a stay in Paris, the ambassador invited Benjamin to La Table d'Eugène, an intimate Michelin-starred restaurant in Montmartre, where the menu was seasonal and dishes could take hours to prepare. Sipping a 2006 Perrier Jouët Belle Epoque, Benjamin learned that Consuela Chavez had recovered the faculty of speech and was working in Paris again. Her bad habits were getting the better of her, and the ambassador predicted a long downhill slide for the once-ravishing woman. Zoltán was awaiting trial in a correctional facility near Budapest. Meanwhile, the vintner impersonators had been apprehended a few days after Viktor and Attila.

On the Rue Eugène Sue, tiny flakes were clinging to the bare trees and the sloped roofs of the eighteenth arrondissement. Benjamin looked up and saw that the snow was coming down faster now. He remembered the bitterly cold days he had spent here not so long ago. Still, Montmartre could be so lovely when it was dressed in white.

Thank you for reading Tainted Tokay.

Please share your thoughts and reactions on your favorite social media and retail platforms.

We love feedback.

ABOUT THE AUTHORS

Noël Balen (left) and Jean-Pierre Alaux (right).
(©David Nakache)

Jean-Pierre Alaux and **Noël Balen** came up with the winemaker detective over a glass of wine, of course. Jean-Pierre Alaux is a magazine, radio, and television journalist when he is not writing novels in southwestern France. The grandson of a winemaker, he has a real passion for food, wine, and winemaking. For him, there is no greater common denominator than wine. Coauthor of the series Noël Balen lives in Paris, where he writes, makes records, and lectures on music. He plays bass, is a music critic, and has authored a number of books about musicians, in addition to many novels and short stories.

www.lefrenchbook.com/alaux-balen/

ABOUT THE TRANSLATOR

Sally Pane studied French at State University of New York Oswego and the Sorbonne before receiving her master's Degree in French Literature from the University of Colorado. Her career includes more than twenty years of translating and teaching French and Italian, and she has translated a number of titles in the Winemaker Detective series. She lives in Boulder, Colorado, with her husband.

www.lefrenchbook.com/our-translators/